A Candlelight
Ecstasy Romance

"ARE YOU TELLING ME YOU DON'T WANT ME TO VISIT YOU IN ATLANTA?"

"Of course not!" Sue exclaimed, a troubled expression on her face. "I'm just trying to give you a way out of all this—if you want it."

"Maybe you're the one who wants a way out," Jared suggested harshly. "Maybe you've decided it's too much trouble having a relationship with a man whose son creates complications."

"That's unfair and you know it," she retorted. "I care about both of you!"

His expression softened. "I care about you, too, Sue, very much. I'm just asking if you want to see me again after we leave the ranch and I return to New York."

"That's up to you," she replied, her uncertainties replacing her anger.

"And that's an evasive answer. If you make up your mind before we leave, let me know," he said as he turned away from her. Then he was gone.

CANDLELIGHT ECSTASY ROMANCES®

DREAM MAKER

Donna Kimel Vitek

A CANDLELIGHT ECSTASY ROMANCE®

Published by
Dell Publishing Co., Inc.
1 Dag Hammarskjold Plaza
New York, New York 10017

Dell ® TM 681510, Dell Publishing Co., Inc.

Candlelight Ecstasy Romance®, 1,203,540, is a registered
trademark of Dell Publishing Co., Inc., New York, New York.

ISBN: 0-440-12155-8

Printed in the United States of America

First printing—March 1986

10 9 8 7 6 5 4 3 2 1

WFH

Listen to the makers of dreams
for they are the guardians of wonder.

—Flavia

To Our Readers:

We have been delighted with your enthusiastic response to Candlelight Ecstasy Romances®, and we thank you for the interest you have shown in this exciting series.

In the upcoming months we will continue to present the distinctive sensuous love stories you have come to expect only from Ecstasy. We look forward to bringing you many more books from your favorite authors and also the very finest work from new authors of contemporary romantic fiction.

As always, we are striving to present the unique, absorbing love stories that you enjoy most—books that are more than ordinary romance. Your suggestions and comments are always welcome. Please write to us at the address below.

Sincerely,

The Editors
Candlelight Romances
1 Dag Hammarskjold Plaza
New York, New York 10017

To Our Readers:

We love to hear from you, and your continued sup-
port is what keeps us going. Your questions and re-
quests help us to improve and tailor our titles to fit
your needs.

In this [...] [...] of the [...] we have some
[...] that you can expect [...] you have come to
[...] only from us. [...] the book lovers, the
[...], and the very best work from new and
[...] and [...] romance authors.

[...] would [...] of [...] the reading
[...] [...] at [...] [...] we bring you [...]—
[...] and romance the way we want it and
[...] it [...] the way it should be.

Sincerely,

The Editors
[...] Romances
A Dell Imprint from [...]

CHAPTER ONE

The moon was a pale golden sliver in the clear Texas sky as Sue Austin drove up to the old homestead. The ranch house was dark, as she had expected it to be. It was after midnight, and her brother Jace and his wife, Leah, weren't expecting her to arrive until tomorrow.

After parking her car and removing her luggage, Sue quietly shut the door and walked to the front porch, unlocking the door with her own key. Noiselessly, she went inside, not wanting to awaken Leah and Jace. There was no need to drag them out of bed when she could simply go to her old room and see them in the morning after a good night's rest.

Even in the shadowy darkness the house was so familiar that she easily made her way down the hall, where she secured the strap of her tote bag over her right shoulder, then turned the doorknob slowly without making a sound. After stepping into her room, she closed the door behind her before switching on the overhead light. A small startled cry escaped her when a strange man suddenly sat up in her bed, the sheet falling down to expose his naked chest.

"Who the devil are you?" he demanded, shielding his eyes with one hand as he glared at her.

Her heart galloping, Sue hastily replied, "I'm Sue —Sue Austin, Jace's sister. I didn't know they had a guest. I mean, I decided not to wake them just to tell them I got here early. You see, I drove down from Atlanta and planned to spend tonight in a motel along the way. But I changed my mind and drove straight through instead. I didn't want to bother them, so I thought I'd just go to bed. I had no idea you were in here."

"Obviously," the man said, raking his hand through his dark blond hair. His eyes becoming accustomed to the bright light, he regarded Sue. "This is your room, I presume?"

"Well, yes, but—"

"Would you like me to sleep on the sofa?"

"Oh no, stay where you are," Sue said. "I can sleep next door. It's no problem."

"I'm afraid it is. My son's in there."

"Then I'll take the sewing room. It has a very comfortable sofa."

"But—"

"I don't mind, really. It is very comfortable. Besides, I'm not going to run you out of a warm bed just because I got here a day early."

"Okay, you talked me into it," the man said. "I'd volunteer to sleep with my son, but he flops around so much, it would be like going to bed in a blender."

12

Sue laughed softly. "I wouldn't think of putting you through an ordeal like that."

"Of course, there's another alternative." A quirk of a smile appeared on the man's firmly sculpted mouth. "We can share this bed."

He was clearly teasing, flirting a little. She didn't mind. "Thanks, but no thanks. Maybe some other time, after we get to know each other better," she retorted saucily, reopening the door to move out into the hallway, where she added in a whisper, "Sorry I disturbed you."

Then she closed the door before he had a chance to answer and made her way to the sewing room, realizing too late that she hadn't even asked him who he way. But at that moment she was too weary to really care. She'd find out tomorrow anyway.

Sue slept until ten the next morning and awoke feeling great, her energy restored. The bone weariness she had felt from the long drive from Atlanta had made her sleep deeply, and she hummed softly to herself as she threw back the lightweight green afghan covering her and got up. After a leisurely shower in the bathroom down the hall, she returned to the sewing room, still humming as she dressed in gray corduroy slacks and a loosely knit white pullover sweater. Before the full-length mirror attached to one wall, she brushed her chestnut hair, then applied a hint of blush to her cheeks and enhanced already long lashes with sable brown mascara. As she put on dusty rose lipstick, she studied her reflection. Her blue eyes shone with excitement, which was no surprise. The first half of December had dragged by, but at last the days had passed, and now she looked forward to two glorious weeks of Christmas vacation with her family, away from her thirty-one fourth-graders. She loved teaching, but nine- and ten-year-old children could be rowdy, a fact that made holidays a sheer necessity of life, if only to preserve sanity. And they needed time away from her, too. When they resumed classes in January, they would all be ready to face new challenges.

As she flicked her hair back over her shoulders, her stomach growled, reminding her that she hadn't eaten anything since the previous evening, when she'd stopped along the way for a light dinner. She decided she'd have a glass of juice, toast with marmalade, and a couple of the fresh eggs that Leah's chickens provided every day.

After slipping her feet into her leather espadrilles, Sue walked down the hall toward the kitchen but stopped in the doorway when she saw her sister-in-law sitting at the wooden table in the middle of the large cheery room, totally absorbed in studying a page in a recipe book. Sue smiled fondly. Jace had been married to Leah for about a year and a half, and she was the best thing that had ever happened to him. He wasn't ashamed to admit she made his life complete and had erased the disillusionment that had resulted from his brief first marriage to Erica. Except on rare occasions he was too much the gentleman to express the criticisms he could have of his ex-wife. But Sue, the protective, loving sister, knew all to well what a dismal wife Erica had been, too selfish to be happy on a Texas ranch. Thank God Leah was the complete opposite, just what Jace

14

needed: a warm and giving, thoughtful and intelligent woman with a sense of humor. And, unlike Erica, she could find pleasure and excitement in the little things in life. Sue loved her like a sister.

"Beautiful morning, isn't it?" she said from the doorway, grinning as Leah turned in her chair, then rose to her feet to dash over and give Sue a hug and kiss on the cheek. Sue kissed her back, then jokingly complained, "Of course, I've missed most of it. You should have made me get up earlier."

"No way." Leah shook her head, her honey blond hair swaying with the motion. "I figured you needed all the sleep you could get after driving straight through from Atlanta. And Jace is likely to give you a sermon because you did. When we got up this morning and saw your car outside, he wasn't a bit happy that you hadn't stopped at a motel for the night."

Sue dismissed that news with a grin and a flippant wave of her hand. "Oh, you know how he is. Trying to play daddy again. He's always been overprotective. You know that."

"I know he loves you very much. We both do," Leah countered. "Why didn't you wake us up when you got in last night?"

"It was late and there was no point in getting you out of bed. Besides, I was so tired, all I wanted to do was sack out myself. But I feel great now, and hungry as a bear. That coffee smells delicious."

"Pour yourself a cup while I make you some breakfast. What would you like?"

"I've got my heart set on toast and marmalade and some eggs, but I can make it myself."

"You will not."

15

"But—"

"Just sit down and relax," Leah persisted, donning a yellow apron. "This is the first real day of your vacation. You deserve breakfast served to you. After today you can be on your own in the mornings. Deal?"

"Deal." Smiling, Sue sat down at the table, idly feathering the corners of the pages of the morning paper with her thumb as she watched her sister-in-law move from the refrigerator to the pantry adjoining the kitchen. When she opened that door, the spicy aromas of cinnamon and nutmeg and ginger wafted out before she returned with two slices of bread. Sue's stomach growled once again as she said, "Speaking of that brother of mine, I guess he's out with Buddy and the hands?"

Leah nodded as she broke one egg into a bowl. "He thought you'd sleep late, and the hands needed help driving the cattle down from the high pastures. The weather man is predicting a cold spell, maybe even snow by tomorrow afternoon. They couldn't leave the herd spread out, in case we have to haul hay out to the cattle. But he'll be here early for lunch, I'm sure. He can't wait to see you."

"It has been a long time. At least six months," Sue conceded rather wistfully. "I've missed you guys. But now that I'm here, you and I have time for a nice long chat. I'm so glad I was able to get here on a Sunday, since you don't have to go in to your studio."

"Believe it or not, I won't have to go in for the next two weeks," Leah informed her with a grin. "I started my own holiday yesterday afternoon. After

16

all, it's Christmas, and I want us all to spend as much time as possible together."

"Oh, that's great," Sue said enthusiastically before taking a sip of the coffee she'd poured for herself. "Maybe we can even convince Jace to let Buddy handle the ranch."

"I'm sure we can."

"I'm sure *you* can; he's like putty in your hands," Sue replied teasingly. "Oh, when I got here last night, I went to my old room, not knowing it was already occupied. Who's that man—"

Before she could finish voicing her question, the very man entered the kitchen by way of the back door. Carrying a basketful of freshly laid eggs, he handed them to Leah and smiled warmly before his gaze focused on Sue, his dark gray eyes taking in the satiny sheen of her chestnut hair, her blue eyes, her slim yet generously curved body. She had looked tired last night, with pale violet crescents forming semicircles beneath her eyes. This morning her delicately etched features were more relaxed, her clear blue eyes aglow with vivacity and curiosity.

Sue and the mystery man looked at each other for several seconds.

Leah chuckled. "You two met last night, I know. But you weren't formally introduced. Sue, this is Jared Ryder, my cousin. Jared, my sister-in-law, Sue."

Her cousin nodded. "Yes, she told me."

With a smile Sue put down her cup and extended a hand. "I'm pleased to meet you—officially. Sorry I woke you last night."

"No problem," was Jared's gracious answer as he returned her firm handshake.

As he poured a cup of coffee for himself, Sue took a better look at him. A bit taller than average, trim and muscular without being the least bit musclebound, Jared had a strong face, and his features were finely carved. His eyes, when he turned and glanced over at her, were dark gray, an unusual color that she found quite attractive, and his skin was lightly tanned although it was winter. Sitting down at the table, he asked her to pass the cream pitcher, and as he took it from her, the tips of his long fingers grazed hers.

"Jared's from New York," Leah said conversationally. "He and Tommy—that's his son—just decided to come down for Christmas a week ago. Nearly knocked my socks off when he called. I've invited him to the ranch dozens of times, but he's always been too busy. Or so he said."

Jared winked teasingly at his cousin. "I wasn't making up excuses, Leah. I really couldn't get away until now."

Sue toyed absently with her napkin. "What do you do in New York, Jared?"

"I publish computer software."

"Oh, really? That's interesting. Do you publish any educational material?"

"Yes, along with business systems, games, and word processing systems, among others."

"I asked about the educational programs because I'm a grammar school teacher. My students love the time they get to spend working with the computers."

"That's music to my ears. Today's children are tomorrow's consumers. I just hope their interest in computers continues," he said with a grin. "Of course, it's nice to know I'm doing something to stimulate young minds, too. Kids don't seem to be as wary of computers as many adults are. Tommy loves to play with ours."

Sue smiled. "How old is Tommy?"

"Seven."

"Ah, that's a nice age," she murmured thoughtfully, wondering why he didn't mention a wife. Was he divorced or a widower? It wouldn't be polite to ask, so she merely continued to look at him.

"I'm divorced," he said rather tersely, holding her gaze.

She almost blushed. Obviously, something in her expression had told him what she was thinking, and she didn't want to seem like a busybody. "I'm sorry, I—"

Her words broke off when the back door suddenly flew open and a small whirlwind entered the room. A blond-haired boy catapulted into the kitchen, his young face scrunched up, tears welling in his big gray-green eyes. "I tried to pick up a chicken. I wanted to p-pet it," he sobbed, holding out his right hand. "It w-was mean and bit me."

"Oh, sweetheart, you got pecked?" Leah exclaimed sympathetically. "I love my chickens, but I know they're not the brightest creatures. Silly things, most of the time. And it was a bad chicken that pecked you, Tommy." She kneeled on the floor and stretched her arm out. "Come here; let me see what that nasty old hen did to you."

For an instant Tommy allowed her to touch his scarcely wounded hand. Then he jerked back, stared wide-eyed for a second at Sue, and at last darted toward his father, crying, "You look at it, Daddy. It hurts."

"Yes. But we'll fix it right up. It'll feel better in a minute," Jared said, comforting his son. Taking Tommy's uninjured hand, Jared led him out of the kitchen.

"Poor little fellow." A tiny frown creased Sue's brow. "Leah?"

"What?"

"Tommy's a beautiful little boy, but I got the feeling that—well, he didn't want you to touch him for very long. And he looked at me as if I scared him. Or am I just imagining things?"

"I wish you were," Leah answered sadly, carrying Sue's eggs and toast to her. Wiping her hands over her apron, she shook her head. "Poor Tommy hasn't had a very easy time of it."

"Oh? Because his parents are divorced?"

"Where Tommy's concerned that's not the half of it," Leah muttered. "Jared's wife left him when Tommy was about three. Found herself another man and didn't want to have to bother with a child. She left Tommy with Jared and hasn't even made an effort to see him since. After that kind of rejection, it's not surprising he's uncomfortable around young women."

Sue shook her head disbelievingly. "How could any mother leave a beautiful child like that?"

"Pure selfishness."

"Sounds a little like Erica."

"Worse. Paula gave Jared hell and then deserted her own son. You can't get much more selfish than that. I feel so sorry for that boy. It's obvious he re-

20

members, at least subconsciously, that his mother ran out on him, and now he's afraid to let himself get close to any young woman. Since they've been here I've tried to get him to trust me a little. No luck. You saw what just happened."

"You keep saying he shies away from young women. What about older ones?"

"He's fine with them, probably because he adores Jared's mother and she worships him. It's just women under forty who put him on edge. He sort of withdraws into himself, and Jared's worried about the effect it might be having on him."

"I can imagine. Maybe seeing a child psychologist would help."

"He's taking him to one. The psychologist is in her late fifties, so Tommy trusts her, but it'll take some time before he can allow himself to really share all those feelings he keeps bottled up inside."

"He won't even talk to his father about it?"

"A little." Leah shrugged. "Jared says he'll make a remark about his mother once in a while, but he clams right up when he tries to get Tommy to talk more about her."

Sue sighed, feeling sorry for both the father and son, especially the child. She couldn't erase the memory of Tommy's gray-green eyes and cornsilk hair, and the searching expression she had seen in his face. Her heart went out to him.

After eating and washing her dishes, Sue left Leah in the kitchen and walked to the front of the ranch house, where she gazed out one of the three small windows in the door, her thumbs hooked in the back pockets of her slacks. The wind picked up and rattled the bare branches of the cottonwoods and oaks, bringing back many a memory of the winters of her childhood. Some people might consider this place too desolate, but she loved it and it was good to be back again, even for a short two weeks.

As she looked outside at the front yard, she noticed something moving out of the corner of her eye. Turning her head, she saw Tommy playing on the porch, carefully removing tiny cars from a worn shoebox and arranging them in neat rows. Her eyes brightened. Opening the coat closet in the hall, she pulled out a lined denim jacket, knowing Leah wouldn't mind if she borrowed it.

Executing her plan, she went outside and walked across the porch, acting for all the world as if she didn't even notice the little boy playing at one end. Although she was well aware of him jerking his head up to stare warily at her, Sue ambled down the steps and across the yard, heading for the swing suspended from a thick, sturdy branch of one of the oaks. She grasped the ropes and got comfortable in the seat, then began pumping her legs under and out until she was flying high. The air was frosty and a low wind blew, lifting her hair off her shoulders and adding more color to her cheeks. It was exhilarating and she enjoyed herself, although she still had a definite purpose in mind as she continued swinging back and forth, her toes dipping toward the ground, then quickly pointing to the sky again. After ten minutes had passed, she wondered if her ploy was a complete failure. But she held back a secret smile when Tommy Ryder began to wander slowly in her direction.

"Oh. Hi," she said blandly when he finally reached the trunk of the tree and started picking off slivers of bark. He didn't really look at her, but she had prepared herself for the silent treatment and decided to handle it by remaining silent herself for another minute or two. When she saw Tommy had lifted his head and was watching her with interest, she glanced casually at him to ask matter-of-factly, "Do you like to swing?"

He simply shrugged.

"Does that mean you don't?"

"I—like to."

"Me too. Tell you what—push me for a while, then I'll let you have a turn and I'll push you. That's the fair way to do it, right?"

"I guess," the child conceded, moving around her as she slowed to a stop. He took the rough lengths of rope in both hands. "Wanna go high?"

"High as the sky," Sue answered, thrilled he'd decided to talk to her, yet determined not to show it. "Push hard."

Tommy did his best, and she soared upward and dipped back down for three or four minutes before she announced, "Okay. It's your turn now."

After he let her slow to a stop and she slipped off the swing, Tommy struggled to lift himself up onto the smooth wooden seat. Her fingers itched to help him, but she restrained herself and let him do it all on his own. When she started pushing him, she didn't touch him at first, pulling the swing back by the ropes, then letting it go. After a while she laid her hands on his shoulders and felt him stiffen momen-

23

tarily, but she didn't give up, and in a few seconds he relaxed again.

"Having fun?" she asked nonchalantly several minutes later. "Or am I pushing you too hard?"

"No. Higher," he demanded, his voice a sweet treble. "Higher."

She honored his request, pleased he was talking to her at all. But she didn't want to push her luck and at last slowed him to a halt. "Brrrr, it's cold out here," she announced, rubbing her hands together. "I think I'll go in and take a hot shower. See you later."

"Wait," the little boy called after her as she started to walk away. "What's your name?"

"Sue. What's yours?"

"Tommy."

"Well, see you later, Tommy," she said lightly, continuing toward the house. She was delighted he'd asked her name and wanted to sweep him up in her arms, yet she knew he would have put up quite a fight if she'd even tried to do that, so she stuck to her plan.

Standing on the front porch, Jared Ryder had witnessed the last two minutes of his son's initial encounter with Sue Austin, and he was surprised. Tommy was actually talking to her, and that in itself was nearly a miracle. The boy usually refused to relate to any young woman. Jared's gray eyes narrowed. Obviously Sue Austin was different as far as Tommy was concerned. But why?

Head bent, pleased by the bit of progress she had made, Sue ran lightly up the steps onto the porch, practically running into Jared, who reached out to grasp her arms before the collision could occur.

"Oh! Sorry," she murmured, lifting her eyes to meet his. "I wasn't looking where I was going."

He dropped his hands, his penetrating gaze plumbing the depths of her eyes. "That's all right," he said quietly, his voice deep. "But tell me how you did it. How did you get my son to talk to you? It's hard to explain, but he doesn't like younger women and—"

"I know," she softly interrupted. "Leah explained it to me."

"Then how did you manage to get him even to talk to you?"

"I pretended to be indifferent to him," she explained with a slight shrug. "I thought he might be more responsive to a woman who didn't want to mother him. You know, reverse psychology."

Jared's dark brown eyebrows shot up. "You could have a point there."

"Maybe. We'll see." Compassion shadowed her features. "I'm just sorry that—"

"No pity, all right?" Jared snapped, his strong jaw tightening. "I don't want it or need it."

"I wasn't about to offer you any," she snapped right back, her anger piqued by his rudeness. "I don't feel sorry for you, mister; you're an adult. But Tommy's just a child paying for the mistake you made by marrying a twit. He's not the only one with problems, obviously. You seem to be carrying quite a large chip on your shoulder."

As Sue swept past him to open the front door, Jared turned to watch, noticing the square set of her shoulders and her lifted chin. A rueful smile formed on his lips. She was a feisty woman, yet obviously one with depth. She had impressed Tommy, made him less wary of her, at least. And she was attractive as well as intriguing, an unbeatable combination, Jared thought. It was a shame he wasn't interested in a relationship with any woman. But that was the way it was; the lessons Paula had taught him still lingered.

CHAPTER TWO

When Jace Austin came in for lunch, Jared watched the reunion between brother and sister with interest. Sue kissed his cheek as Jace embraced her in an enthusiastic hug. They affectionately exchanged jesting comments about each other, and it was obvious that they were close. Their relationship was so free and natural that Jared smiled to himself as he leaned against the kitchen counter. He had no sister and knew that was his loss. Having a girl in his family undoubtedly would have enriched his life, and if he had had a sister, perhaps Tommy would've gotten over his distrust of young women; a loving aunt would have proved to him that not all women were as callous and unfeeling as his own mother.

But that was merely wishful thinking on Jared's part. He had only a brother, Matt, who claimed to be a confirmed bachelor, so there wasn't even an aunt by marriage to take Tommy under her wing. A pity, but also a fact of life that Jared couldn't alter. All he could do was continue to try everything possible to help his son overcome his hurt and resentment. Apparently he and the psychologist were making progress; a year ago Tommy wouldn't have gone near Sue, much less allowed her to push him in the swing and actually talk to her.

"Jace, honey, you look half frozen," Leah said, interrupting Jared's thoughts.

"You're warming me up fast," Jace said after he kissed her. "But the wind is raw today."

"Always is on the open range in winter," Sue said, walking back to the sink where she'd been washing lettuce. "I'm going to bundle up when I ride out with you for a while tomorrow."

"Okay if I ride along too?" Jared spoke up. "Sounds interesting."

Sue glanced over her shoulder at him. "If you call freezing your rear end off interesting."

Raising his eyebrows, Jared looked at her steadily, a small smile breaking on his face. "Insinuating I'm a city boy, Ms. Austin?"

"If the shoe fits, Mr. Ryder."

"As a matter of fact, it doesn't. I grew up on a farm in Connecticut, so I can tell you a little about winters. Three feet of snow on the ground, five-foot drifts. And I spent a lot of time outside and survived."

Along with Leah, Jace laughed. "I think he's got you there, sis."

And even Sue had to chuckle good-naturedly as she made an imaginary mark in the air. "I have to admit that's one for you, Jared."

"Ah, now we're back on a first-name basis," he countered, grinning. "That's an improvement."

Sue nodded graciously, but as his gray eyes drifted slowly over her, she recalled his offer last night to share his bed with her and a mild tingle coursed along her spine. Trying to ignore it, she turned back to the sink.

While Jace washed up, Leah and Sue put the finishing touches on the hearty noonday meal as Jared helped by setting the table. He was putting down a fifth stoneware plate when Jace returned and Tommy bounced into the kitchen.

"Cookie said I could eat with the men today," the boy announced, his round face alight with excitement. "Okay, Daddy?"

"Sure," Jared answered, fondly ruffling his son's blond hair. "Sounds like fun. Want me to walk you over?"

Shaking his head, Tommy pulled on the jacket he carried as he ran like a flash to the back door.

The four adults sat down to lunch, everyone digging into the hot Texas chili Leah made to perfection, along with fresh salad and warm home-baked bread. Conversation was relaxed and interesting until Leah suddenly said to her husband, "As it turns out, Sue and Jared have a lot in common."

Sue struggled not to choke on a piece of lettuce as she glanced sideways at Jared, still resenting the tone of voice he'd used with her out on the front porch. At that moment she couldn't imagine what they possibly had in common, and she looked questioningly at her sister-in-law. "Do we?"

"Sure. He publishes computer software and you said your pupils love working with computers. Should give the two of you a lot to talk about. You can tell him what your kids like, and that might even help him develop educational systems. Right, Jared?"

"Could be," he answered, looking steadily at Sue. "I'd certainly be interested in hearing what you have to say on the subject."

"I'm sure my input's not needed," she responded, keeping her tone as light as she could. "You must have marketing researchers who advise you."

He nodded. "True. But you deal with children every day. If you have any suggestions, I really would like to hear them."

"Well, if you're sure . . . I'd love to see discs that were less fragile. After all, you can wipe out most of one simply by forgetting to turn on the disc drive or even with a bit of dust. Grade school children don't always have clean hands."

"That is a problem," he conceded, "and we are working on it. Anything else?"

"Yes. The graphics in the games. Some of them are pathetic—my kids could draw more realistic figures. Not too long ago we received a game program and the hero searching for the lost treasure was no better than a stick drawing."

Jared's eyes narrowed. "Maybe you'd better have a look at some of *our* games before passing judgment on the whole industry. I think our graphics are damned good."

"Happy to," she muttered, forgetting for a moment that Jace and Leah were seated at the table with them, feeling they were alone, sparring with words. If he hadn't been so rude to her earlier, she could never have been so cool to him now. But Sue didn't have to put up with rudeness from any man, no matter how attractive he was. "Just send any of your new educational programs to me, care of Carter Elementary in Atlanta, and I'll look them over."

"Happy to." He repeated her words, then suddenly relaxed, seeing the humor in the situation. They were at odds with each other for no good reason except that he had inexplicably snapped at her outside, and in self-defense she had snapped right back at him. Perhaps it was time to try to make amends. His expression softened as he inclined his head. "I'm serious; your opinion would be very valuable."

Although she sensed his subtle change of attitude, she wasn't quite ready to let up. After all, she had only offered a few words of commiseration, and he had thrown them right back in her face. Yet his mood *had* changed, and the least she could do was try to act polite. "If you think my opinion might be worth anything, I'll be glad to give it."

"Good."

"Fine."

"Carter Elementary, Atlanta? Right?"

"Yes."

Despite the thaw, there was still a certain tension between them, and after Sue finished her chili and touched the napkin to the corners of her mouth, she sat back silently in her chair, observing him out of the corner of her eye.

All the while Jared looked at her. "I'm not kidding."

"I believe you."

"Do you?"

"Shouldn't I?"

Jace Austin coughed to regain their attention. "Sounds like a good idea to me, sis. You could give Jared some good advice."

She looked at her older brother. "I guess," she said flatly. "But will my advice really count?"

On that somewhat strained note, lunch ended. When Sue rose to help Leah clear the table and wash the dishes, the two men donned heavy coats and went outside. A pale sun shone in the clear blue sky, raising the afternoon temperature a few degrees. They approached the bunkhouse, where a spiral of smoke rose from the chimney, and as they reached the foot of the wooden steps that led to the door, Jace stopped short to look at Jared. "What do you think of Sue?" he asked.

"She's intelligent. Funny. Sensitive. Very attractive," Jared easily answered, though a perplexed frown creased his brow. "But why do you ask?"

Jace grinned. "I'm surprised you don't know. Leah's in a matchmaking mood. She thought it might be a good idea to get the two of you together, since you have a lot in common. And Leah's a real romantic—a natural matchmaker."

Sighing, Jared shook his head. "She's barking up the wrong tree this time, I'm afraid. She's a sweetheart, and I like your sister, but I'm not ready to get involved with any woman right now. Someday I'm sure I'll change my mind. But not yet. Paula taught me to be very careful where women are concerned, and I took that lesson to heart. I have no intention of getting into a serious relationship with anyone right now."

32

"Famous last words," Jace calmly remarked. "I was saying the very same thing after Erica and I split up. But there was Leah, and she changed my mind eventually. A man needs a woman in his life."

"Yes, but I can wait. I want to wait. I made one mistake and I sure don't want to make another. Not that I don't think Sue's a fine woman! Don't get me wrong. She's very nice."

"She's the best," Jace proudly proclaimed. "But if the two of you aren't right for each other, that's it. Leah just thought it was a good idea to give it a chance."

Jared grinned. "So that's why she invited Tommy and me down for Christmas?"

"You know better than that. She's been trying to get you to come for a visit since we got married."

Nodding agreeably, Jared followed Jace into the bunkhouse, where a man was adding another split log to the fire in the wood stove that warmed the small building. At the far end the rest of the hands sat around a long table, finishing their meal. Tommy, who sat next to Buddy, the foreman, didn't even notice his father come in. His eyes wide with fascination, he listened intently as the man across from him spun exaggerated yarns about his life as a cowboy.

Unfortunately Buddy had to put a temporary end to the tall tales. Patting Tommy's shoulder, he got up and stepped over the bench, saying in his quiet way, "Okay, men, time to get back to work."

After final swigs of steaming coffee, the ranch hands put on their hats and coats. Tommy noticed Jared at last and ran around the table toward him.

"Guess what? Guess what!" he chattered, gesturing with excitement. "Know what Zeke had to do one time? He had to fight off a big mean grizzly bear all on his lonesome! That means all by himself."

Though he saw the amused winks a few hands exchanged, Jared gazed down at his son, looking suitably impressed. "That's some story. Zeke must be a very brave man."

"Strong, too. That bad old bear tried to grab him and squeeze him, but Zeke picked up a big log and just knocked that bear cockeyed. That means silly. And then—"

Tommy's words broke off abruptly when Sue entered the bunkhouse and was greeted enthusiastically by all the men, especially the foreman and the cook. She gave both Cookie and Buddy big hugs and then spoke to all the other hands individually, saving a teasing grin for a short, wiry man who had chewing tobacco tucked in against one cheek.

"Zeke, you never change a bit. Never look a day older."

"There's a reason for that, Miss Susan," Zeke drawled. "Clean living."

His fellow ranch hands hooted, and Sue herself couldn't suppress a disbelieving smile. "I think maybe you stay young because of that imagination of yours. I'm sure you're still telling those tall tales. Right?"

"How did you guess?" her brother asked. "Zeke entertained Tommy with one of his stories during lunch."

"Oh?" Turning, Sue looked at the boy, wanting to ask which story he'd been told, but instinct kept her silent. Nonaggression had worked with him once already, so she tried for a second minor victory by simply lifting one questioning eyebrow as his gaze made brief contact with hers.

"It was about a bear," Tommy murmured at last. "A mean grizzly bear."

"Oh yes, that one. I remember it." Sue pretended to shiver. "It's really scary, isn't it?"

He nodded. "Yes, ma'am."

"Oh, I don't think you have to call me ma'am, Tommy. Call me Sue or Susan like everybody else does. All right?"

"Okay."

He had spoken only a few words to her, but Sue felt a sense of achievement. It was at least a beginning of interaction that could, with a bit of luck, develop into some semblance of a relationship in which he wouldn't automatically consider her an enemy because of her age and her sex. And when she looked up at Jared and saw the momentary glint of admiration appear in his eye, she was more than pleased.

"Okay, let's mosey on back to the house," he said, turning his attention back to his son. "If you want to stay up until nine tonight, you have to take an afternoon nap. Okay, cowpoke?"

Tommy giggled, started to reach for his father's hand, then changed his mind, apparently remembering he was too old for such things. The ranch hands called good-bye to him while he wiggled into his jacket.

"Zeke, you old devil, I'm going to have to write down all the stories you tell one of these days and make a book of them," Sue commented wryly as father and son left the bunkhouse. Then she waved everybody toward the door. "Don't let me keep you, fellows. I just wanted to come out and say hello. Don't let this brother of mine work you too hard. After all, it's the Christmas season and you shouldn't have to spend all of it with the cattle."

"Don't you worry none," Buddy answered, giving her a slow smile. "Jace is giving all of us four days off sometime during the next two weeks, so you can bet there'll be some hell-raising going on."

" 'Sides, we got all the cattle down from the high pastures, close enough so we can come in where it's warm to eat," one of the younger hands spoke up. "Good thing, too. Cookie don't fix nothing more than beans and bacon for us on the range, and by the time you get them from the plate to your mouth they ain't hot no more, not in this weather. Colder'n a—"

"Cold? You think this is cold?" Zeke interrupted, snorting. "You ain't never seen cold, boy! Did I ever tell you about the winter of '66 when—"

" 'The heels of our boots froze solid to our stir-rups?' " Sue and Jace whispered simultaneously, having heard the story countless times. Trying not to laugh aloud, they left the bunkhouse together.

After Jace and the men had mounted their horses and ridden off, she walked back toward the house. The wind kicked up a mild fuss, swirling dust in the barnyard and parting her hair at her nape to sneak under her collar. This time she shivered for real, but she rubbed her hands up and down her arms briskly to increase her circulation before thrusting them into her jacket pockets. Atlanta was warmer, but home was home, and she still enjoyed the challenge the weather presented, with blazing summers and icy winters.

Leah was on the phone when Sue walked into the kitchen. Unbuttoning her jacket with one hand, she waved with the other at her sister-in-law, then ambled down the hall. When she heard the down-home twang of Willie Nelson on the radio in the den, she stopped. The door was ajar, so she pushed it wider and stood for a long moment, observing Jared as he sat on the sofa, his eyes closed. He wasn't asleep. His chin rested on long steepled fingers, and a thoughtful frown lightly etched his dark brow. Her gaze wandered over him. He was definitely an attractive man, and she guessed he was about thirty-two or thirty-three, somewhere between six and seven years older than she was.

His frown deepened suddenly, then disappeared almost completely, yet she found she couldn't just walk away from him. She couldn't help wondering what he was thinking. About his son, whose sense of security had been undermined by his mother's desertion? Or was he simply listening to the song on the radio? Those questions flicked swiftly through her brain, yet it wasn't curiosity that made her step across the threshold into the den. Something deeper, compassion perhaps, caused her to make a small noise in her throat to gain Jared's attention.

He slowly opened his eyes, then allowed his dark gaze to survey the delicate, prettily drawn features of her wind-flushed face. He inclined his head.

She took another step forward, nodding back. "Looks like you got Tommy to go to sleep."

"Yes. He's still not used to a different time zone. I

guess it takes children his age longer to adapt." Jared's long legs had been outstretched and crossed at the ankles, but now he sat up straighter, combing his fingers through his hair as Sue poised herself on the cushion at the far end of the sofa. He grimaced almost comically. "Look, I want to apologize for snapping at you this morning, about saying I didn't want your pity—although I don't. I guess I'm overly sensitive from seeing too many friends and relatives treating Tommy and me with kid gloves since Paula took off. But after thinking about what you were trying to say, I don't believe you were just feeling sorry for us."

"You're right; I wasn't," she informed him frankly. "I don't pity Tommy or you. You have each other and love each other, which is a lot more than some people have. I *am* sorry that what happened had to happen, but life's not always the way we want it to be. When things go wrong, some people get crushed, but I have a feeling you and Tommy can be strong together and eventually work it all out."

"I think so too. I also think you're very good for him," Jared said. "You don't push him. You wait for him to make the first move. So far, I think you're being successful because you're a surprise to him. All the other young women he's met since Paula left have tried to baby him."

"He is a darling," Sue said softly. "I wouldn't mind babying him myself."

"But you know better. That makes the difference." The muscles in Jared's strong jaw tensed, then he visibly relaxed. "Anyway, I think you're handling him just right. Thanks."

She managed a gracious smile, although the rate of her heartbeat had increased. Deep inside she realized with some wonder that Jared Ryder was affecting her in an unusual way. She had never met a man who made such a good first impression, despite the cross words they had exchanged earlier. Jared was sophisticated yet natural, intelligent yet unassuming, inherently virile and masculine yet so secure in himself he could admit he had made a mistake and offer a sincere apology. She had to admire him.

When she noticed several folders spilling out of a tan briefcase on the end table beside him, she started to stand. "Sorry, I didn't mean to interrupt your work."

He shook his head. "I was pretending to work, but I'm not really in the mood. Reading over contracts can be dull business."

"How did you get into publishing computer software?"

"I persuaded my father that his electronics firm should branch out. We're not a large company, but we're growing."

"Then your work must be very exciting."

"For the most part, yes. But there's always some boring paperwork to catch up on."

Sue grimaced comically. "Tell me about it. Do you know how many papers I grade every week?"

"But you love it," he said perceptively.

"Yes," she admitted, chuckling. "I gripe and complain sometimes, but most teachers do. Still, we'd change professions if we were really unhappy, and I don't plan to do that. The kids make it all worthwhile."

"Just by seeing the way you act around Tommy, I think your students are lucky to have you as a teacher."

"Thank you. But does that mean you think I'm the typical old schoolmarm, strict but big-hearted and just a little homely?"

He laughed. "I didn't say that. You certainly don't fit my mental image of a homely schoolmarm."

"A wise answer," she said jokingly, then changed the subject, wanting to know more about him and his family. "Leah told me you have a younger brother. Is he in business with you and your father?"

"Not Matt. Business leaves him cold. He's something of a free spirit, drifting from job to job, but he's happy and that's what's important."

"Yes. But I don't think I could live that way. I need a more structured life."

"Me too. But that just goes to show that brothers can be totally different."

She nodded agreement, then noticed that somehow, sometime during the past few minutes, Jared had moved closer to her on the sofa. As a pleasant warmth stole over her, she felt compelled to draw back a little. "Well, I won't bother you any longer, since you have contracts to read whether you want to work or not."

"These can wait, and I'm tired of toiling," was his response as he gathered the folders and returned them to the briefcase. "What are you going to do now?"

She shrugged. "I guess I'd better go over my Christmas lists. I'm one of those people who waits until the last minute to shop."

Jared sprang to his feet and followed as she moved gracefully across the den, her dark chestnut hair highlighted with auburn-gold strands. Just as she stepped into the doorway, she stopped, turned back toward him, then rose on tiptoe and touched her lips to his.

"Susan," he murmured, his deep voice lowering.

"Look up," she whispered, pulling back. "See?"

And see he did. The glossy evergreen leaves of mistletoe hung from the lintel above them.

She smiled at him. "Can't defy old traditions, can we?"

"No."

And before she could fully realize what was happening, he drew her close again and his firm, warm lips feathered gently over hers. She had acted on impulse, but his response seemed serious and after a brief, electrically charged instant, she drew away, producing a nonplussed smile. "Well, now that we've done our duty, I'll see you later."

"Yes. Later, Susan."

She moved away and strolled as casually as possible down the hall to the sewing room, the fiery touch of his mouth still lingering on hers.

CHAPTER THREE

Jace, an avid movie buff, provided the evening's entertainment. In the study he hooked up the VCR, then gave Leah, Sue, and Jared the chance to suggest one of the many film cassettes in his collection. Tommy was already tucked in bed and sleeping peacefully.

"After everybody picks one, we'll vote on it," Jace said, dropping down on the sofa. "I wouldn't mind seeing *Star Wars* again. It's been a while."

Leah sat down next to him. "How about *Play It Again, Sam?* I love Woody Allen."

"Me too," Sue murmured, scanning the cassette titles beside Jared for a few moments before nodding. "But I'd rather see *Lilies of the Field*. Sidney Poitier is one of my favorite actors."

"Mine, too, but I feel like something really zany tonight. Ah! *Airplane,*" was Jared's choice. "It's a great spoof."

Leah, Sue, and Jace agreed simultaneously.

Spreading his hands outward, palms up, Jared grinned. "Right. Pure unadulterated escapism. That's what I'm in the mood for. I rest my case."

He had presented it well, and they unanimously agreed on *Airplane*, sharing the outrageous humor as they watched it.

"I'd forgotten how insane it was," Sue commented as the movie ended and the credits rolled. "Whoever wrote the script must be a little strange, in the nicest kind of way."

Although he was chuckling still, Jace suddenly yawned, putting his arm around his wife's shoulders. "Well, this was fun, folks, but I have to get up at the crack of dawn. Ready for bed, honey?"

Glancing indifferently at the empty popcorn bowls and four empty glasses on the coffee table, Leah nodded. "I can clean up in the morning."

"I'll clean up for you now," Sue said. "I'm not very sleepy yet. You two run along. I'll take care of everything."

"I'll help," Jared offered, gathering the glasses as Jace and Leah said good night and headed out of the study.

A short time later Jared dried the glasses and bowls after Sue washed them in sudsy water, then gave them a good rinse. When the chore was completed, they both dried their hands before Sue opened the door to the utility room to toss the damp towel into the laundry basket.

When she walked back toward him, he smiled. "Leah's always been one of my favorite relatives. I'm glad she found a husband like Jace. He's just right for her—a fine man."

"He's the best."

"That's exactly what he said about you."

"Really?" Sue responded curiously. "May I ask why you two were talking about me?"

"He just mentioned that Leah was trying to play matchmaker, hoping to get us together."

Perhaps she should have been embarrassed, but she wasn't. Sue had to laugh.

Jared frowned. "You think that's funny? Why? Am I that unappealing?"

"Oh, it's not that at all. You're very . . ." She shook her head, her laughter dying away. "It's just that Leah's such a romantic. Imagine her trying to get us together just because she's happily married. I mean, you and I aren't the kind of people who can be manipulated even by somebody who loves us. What did you say to Jace when he let you in on her little secret?"

"I said I wasn't interested," was Jared's answer.

"Oh," she muttered, somewhat stung by his bluntness. "At least you're honest."

"It has nothing to do with you, Sue. It's just that I was burned once and I have no desire to jump into the fire again anytime soon."

His compelling gray eyes held hers, and her heart did some crazy acrobatics as she looked up at him, then away, deciding it was time to turn the conversation in a different direction. "I'm surprised you came here for Christmas," she said, blurting out the first thing that came into her mind. "Since Tommy's so close to your parents, especially your mother, why aren't you spending the holidays with them?"

"They deserted us," he answered with an under-

44

standing smile. "They're celebrating their thirty-fifth anniversary on December twentieth, and since they spent their honeymoon in Paris, Matt and I chipped in to send them back this year. They jumped at the chance. When we saw them off at the airport, they were acting like newlyweds."

"Oh, that's nice," Sue said, her tone wistful. "It's so good to realize some marriages turn out right and last for years and years. My parents were like that. They were devoted to each other. In fact, after my mother died, I think my father actually pined away in grief, he missed her so much. And I think Jace and Leah have a marriage like that."

"So do I," Jared said, then gave a brief nod of his head. "Well, I think I'll go bundle Tommy up so he won't get cold when we go over to Leah's old house."

"What are you talking about?" Sue exclaimed softly, thoroughly perplexed. "Why are you going over there?"

"Well, the tenant moved out a month ago, so it's empty. We can't make you sleep in the sewing room for the next two weeks."

"But I don't mind, really. It's comfortable. You don't have to go over—"

"I won't keep you out of your old bed," Jared persisted, his chiseled features becoming more angular with insistence. "Besides, Leah showed Tommy and me her house and he loved it. He wants us to move over there."

Sue's face fell. "Do you think he just wants to get away from Leah and me?"

"That could be part of it," Jared told her honestly, then added, "but mostly he likes the house, especially upstairs. Maybe it reminds him of the farm-house in Connecticut."

"I feel like I'm running you and Tommy out of here and—"

"But you're not. It was my choice. And his," Jared stated firmly, turning away from her to start toward the kitchen door. "It's late. I'd better get Tommy and go."

Sue took a swift step after him. "At least let me drive you over there. It's cold outside, and if you have to carry Tommy all that way, he might wake up, especially if you have to shift him around to get the door open. I'll take you over."

"Not a bad idea," Jared agreed easily. "Meet you outside in a minute or two."

It was a short ride along the ranch drive, across the road, and up the gentle rise beside the house Leah had lived in before marrying Jace. Taking the key, Sue went ahead to unlock the side door that led into the kitchen. As she leaned inside to switch on the light, Jared joined her in the doorway, holding Tommy in his arms.

"This is a first for me," he said, speaking barely above a whisper as he smiled at Sue. "I've never had a woman escort me home before."

She smiled back.

"Thanks for bringing us over."

"No trouble," she murmured, looking at his sleeping son. His fine hair curved across his forehead, and she touched it lightly with her fingertips, loving its soft texture. On impulse she leaned down and gently kissed his rounded cheek before returning her gaze to his father. "I'd never get away with that if he were awake."

"Not yet, anyway," Jared agreed, then wryly cocked one eyebrow. "But what about dear old Dad? Don't you have a good-night kiss for me?"

She decided he was kidding. "Not yet, anyway," she echoed his words before walking back to the car.

Tommy and Jared spent their days on the ranch. Tuesday morning Sue found them in the kitchen, where the boy was having a mid-morning snack of milk and home-baked sugar cookies. When he looked up to say hello and actually gave her a tentative smile, she responded in a subdued manner despite her urge to hug him. But she didn't want to risk reversing the slow but sure progress she felt she was making in their relationship, so when she sat down at the table, she gave her attention to Jared.

"How'd you like riding out with the hands yesterday?" she asked. "Have fun?"

"At first, but the sense of adventure didn't last," he confessed, smiling ruefully. "After about four hours I was ready to come back to a warm fire. Like you said, I nearly froze my rear end off."

"But you said you're used to harsh winters."

"I'm used to snow and cold temperatures. Not a whipping wind over open plains."

"Well, you survived."

"I think so. Although I'm not sure my buns didn't get a little frostbite."

Laughing merrily, she met his eyes. "You know, you seem like a very nice man."

"I'm going to take that as a compliment," he said

47

with a chuckle. "Although it certainly sounded like it might be a backhanded one. Still miffed at me for being such a grouch the other day on the porch?"

"No."

"But?"

"But nothing."

"Come on, tell the truth," he persisted. "You do have something to complain about where I'm concerned, don't you?"

"No," she lied, unwilling to admit she thought it was grossly unfair for him to judge all women unfavorably simply because his ex-wife was a fool. Such an admission would be too revealing, telling him that she wouldn't mind getting involved with him if such an involvement was meant to be. Since he had already stated in no uncertain terms than he didn't want a relationship with any woman, including her, Sue didn't want to do anything to make it appear she was chasing him. She shrugged. "I have no complaints."

"Sure?"

"Positive."

"Look, Susan, I—"

Before he could finish speaking, Tommy drained the milk from his glass and asked, "Daddy, can I go see Cookie now? He said I could help him make dinner for the hands and I want to show him all my cars. Okay?"

"Sure, go ahead," Jared said, shifting his gaze slowly from Sue to his son. "Just don't drop any of those cars into the biscuit dough. Metal's awfully hard to chew, you know."

Tommy laughed. "Oh, Daddy."

48

"Be sure to wear your jacket," Sue called after the boy when he dashed away, then felt like biting her tongue the instant the words were out of her mouth. When Tommy glanced back at her with some surprise, she weakly added, "Your dad doesn't want you to have a bad cold at Christmas."

The child didn't answer, but he did pull his coat down off a peg next to the back door and put it on, zipping it all the way up as he went outside.

Sue shook her head. "Damn, that just slipped out. I'm so used to saying the same thing to my fourth-graders."

Jared shrugged. "No harm done as far as I could tell. Tommy didn't seem to mind. You don't have to handle him with kid gloves, Susan. Just carefully."

Leah walked into the kitchen then, a faint frown marking her brow. "I knew I'd be lucky to get two whole weeks of vacation," she grumbled, then explained. "I just got a call from one of my best customers. Her sister and her family are in Dallas for the holidays, and Dottie begged me to come into the studio just long enough to take a portrait of the whole clan."

"Couldn't you have just said no?" Sue asked.

"I really would have felt bad if I'd refused. Dottie's sister lives in Canada and they get together only every three or four years. Besides, Dottie's a friend." Leah reached for her purse and quilted down coat. "Sue, tell Jace I had to go to the studio for a while. As for lunch . . ."

"Don't worry about a thing. I'll take care of it."

"Well, there's a casserole in the refrigerator ready to be popped into the oven. I'll let you decide what to

49

have along with it." Leah started out, stopped, then turned back to them. "I'm sorry to run out on you like this, Jared. But Sue will entertain you while I'm gone, won't you, Sue? If you want to look around the ranch, she'll be a much better guide than I am anyway. She knows every inch of this place, and I'm still learning. Well, I hope I won't be gone too long. See you."

Leah rushed out the door, obviously wanting to get to her studio, accomplish her task, and get back home as soon as possible. Left alone in the kitchen, Sue and Jared looked at each other for several seconds before he reached across the table to lay one hand over hers. "You heard her—she wants you to entertain me. What kind of entertainment do you suggest?"

"How about baking lessons?" she asked, unable to suppress a small smile as she slipped her hand out from beneath his. "I have just enough time to bake cinnamon buns for Jace—they're one of his favorite sweets. Maybe you'd like to learn how to make them?"

"I'm game for anything," he said, standing as she did. "And it may surprise you to know that I'm no stranger to kitchens. Tommy and I go home to the farm on the weekends, but during the week we live in an apartment in the city. I had to learn how to cook a long time ago. You can't raise a child on TV dinners."

"Then making cinnamon buns should be a snap," she replied dryly, getting a mixing bowl from one of the cabinets. "Now why don't you get the flour and sugar—in those canisters over there."

By the time the baking lesson ended, Sue had yet another reason to admire Jared. He disproved the silly myth that men are useless in a kitchen by becoming an equal partner instead of a student apprentice. After she rolled out the dough, brushed melted butter over it and sprinkled on cinnamon, he rolled it up, cut it in slices, then put it aside to rise while she put the casserole into the oven and fixed the vegetables.

Lunch was delicious. Sue, Jared, and Jace ate heartily. Tommy didn't join them, having decided to take his meal with the hands who had become real-life heroes to him, thanks in part to Zeke's tall tales.

"Little fellow doesn't know what he's missing," Jace said before savoring the first bite of a warm cinnamon bun. "Cookie's feeding them steak and potatoes again, with tapioca pudding for dessert if they're lucky. Or maybe I should say unlucky. Anyway, Tommy's going to be sorry he missed these buns. They're great, sis."

"We'll save him some. And thanks, but I can't take all the credit," Sue confessed, grinning. "Jared helped make them."

"Then my compliments to the chefs," said Jace, reaching for another bun after finishing the first, that action a compliment in itself.

Fifteen minutes later Jared walked out to the bunkhouse to get Tommy, whose crestfallen expression when he saw him wasn't exactly a welcome mat. His small face screwed up into a pouty scowl. "Daddy, I'm helping Cookie wash dishes."

"Okay, but you have to go in for your nap soon."

"But I'm not sleepy. Honest. And Cookie hasn't

looked at my cars yet. Let me stay awhile longer, Daddy. *Please?*"

Defeated by his only child's charm, Jared shook his head in resignation and looked at the cook. "Sure you don't mind if he stays?"

"Glad to have him. I like to talk, and he's a mighty good listener. Zeke's not the only one's got stories to tell. I got a few myself, and little Tom here likes to hear 'em. I'll take good care of him, Mr. Ryder."

"Call me Jared, Cookie."

"Can I stay, Daddy?" Tommy piped up, his bright gray-green eyes showing he knew the answer before he asked the question. "I'm not sleepy. Really."

Nodding his permission, Jared consulted his wristwatch and said, "You can stay, but only until three o'clock. I'll come back to get you then because you have to take a nap before dinner. If you don't, you'll be crotchety all evening. Deal?"

Bobbing his head, Tommy flashed a wide grin.

When Jared stepped back into the kitchen a few minutes later, he found that Sue was no longer there. Taking the initiative, he strode down the hallway that led to the bedrooms and rapped his knuckles lightly on her door. She answered quickly, her gaze drifting past him.

"Where's Tommy?" she asked. "Already in bed for his nap?"

"No, the little devil conned me into postponing it," was Jared's wry answer as his eyes wandered slowly over her. She looked terrific in faded denim jeans and a loose sweater that covered but couldn't conceal her generously uprising breasts. Desire stirred in him, and for the first time since long before his

52

wife had left, Jared experienced a need for a woman that transcended mere physical longing. His response to Sue was deeper than that; emotion was involved. In her he suspected he might find a kindred spirit. He felt younger suddenly, remembering that relationships between men and women—really satisfying relationships—had to offer much more than good sex. It seemed to him that Sue could give a great deal more than that.

As his gaze traveled over her from the top of her head to the tips of her toes, Sue's heartbeat accelerated to a racing thump. She knew that look on his face; she had seen it before and conditioned herself to ignore it. But she couldn't ignore Jared, perhaps because his lean features seemed to express more than mere physical need. There was something else there. Or was she simply imagining that? She didn't think so. He wasn't a shallow man; she already knew that much about him.

"So my son's deserted me," he said softly, ending the intensifying silence between them with a hopeful smile. "And since Leah left you in charge of entertainment, entertain me, Sue."

She drew in a deep breath, then nodded, trying to appear nonchalant. "Okay. Leah suggested a tour of the ranch. I can show you the barn, though I'm afraid it's not what you'd call exciting. But at least we'd have a nice walk."

"Why don't we go riding instead?" he suggested. "I think that would be more fun."

Her eyebrows rose. "You know how to ride?"

Throwing his hands up, he shook his head admonishingly. "When are you going to stop assuming I'm a

53

city slicker? Yes, I know how to ride. We do have horses in Connecticut, and I've been riding since I can remember. I think I can handle it . . . unless you plan to give me a wild mustang that hasn't been broken yet."

Pretending to be disappointed, she snapped her fingers. "I'm afraid we have only wild horses out in the barn. We Texans love a challenge. Once a horse is tame, it's no fun to us anymore."

"Funny," he murmured dryly, his smile deepening as they went to the kitchen, put on their coats, and walked out into the cold air. The endless sky was overcast with brooding gray clouds, and fat wet snowflakes drifted down.

"Crazy weather," Sue remarked as they walked to the barn. "It doesn't snow much here, but this is the second time this winter, according to Leah."

"Seems like it's going to be a cold season for most of the country. Hope it's not quite as severe as it was last year. We got two feet of snow on the farm overnight."

"We had terrible ice storms in Atlanta that nearly shut the city down. Southern towns aren't prepared to cope with those kinds of conditions."

As Jared opened the barn doors, he looked at Sue. She looked at him. They burst out laughing in unison and she shook her head incredulously. "I can't believe we're talking about the weather. I'm sure there must be something more interesting for us to discuss."

"Absolutely," he agreed while they walked along the stalls. "Why don't you tell me why you decided to leave Texas."

Sue vetoed that idea. "Oh, my reasons aren't at all exciting, and I wouldn't want to bore you with them."

"Try me."

"Maybe later." Sue stopped before a stall door and reached across to rub a roan stallion's velvety nose. "This is Lookout. You'll enjoy riding him; he's energetic but hardly a wild mustang."

"Good. I'm not interested in becoming a bronc buster."

Grinning, Sue moved to the next stall to say hello to a sleek black mare with a stark white marking in the center of her forehead. The horse whinnied an affectionate welcome before nudging Sue's hand with her nose. "No, girl, I didn't bring you a carrot this time. Sorry, I won't forget again." She looked up at Jared. "This is Teeny-Bop."

"Teeny-Bop?" Curiosity mantled his lean features. "With that marking I'm surprised she's not named Star."

She waved one hand. "Too ordinary. Give me credit for more imagination than that."

"Ah, you're the one who named her? Why Teeny-Bop?"

A sudden sadness darkened Sue's blue eyes before she looked at Jared. "I named her that because she was born just after Dad died and that was his nickname for me. I thought calling the foal Teeny-Bop would be another way of remembering him."

Jared's gray eyes held hers. He lifted one arm to brush the hair-rough back of his hand along the high-boned contour of her cheek. "I'm sorry about your parents, Susan," he said quietly, his compassionate

55

gaze locking with hers. "Leah told me you and Jace lost both of them within a couple of years. That must have been very hard for both of you."

"Maybe harder for Jace than for me," she suggested, her tone subdued. "He felt responsible for me when Dad died so soon after Mom. He resigned his commission in the Navy and came home to take care of me and the ranch. I've always felt a little guilty about that."

"I can understand your feeling that way, but I doubt you should. Jace is a strong, independent man. He came home because he wanted to. Besides, if he hadn't, he wouldn't have found Leah. And it's obvious she makes him very happy."

"True," Sue agreed, forcing herself to perk up and smile again as she led Jared to the tack room, where they gathered saddles and reins.

Several minutes later they led Lookout and Teeny-Bop out of the barn, mounted the eager horses, and settled comfortably in the saddle. Huge flakes of snow landed in Sue's hair where it escaped her hat, creating sparkling diadems of ice in the thick chestnut tresses. The chilly air was invigorating; she breathed it in, smelling the country freshness, then smiled her joy at Jared before glancing around.

"There's really not much to see on a ranch," she told him. "I mean, most of it is grazing land, with some brown scrub brush thrown in to break the monotony. Why don't we ride across the road into the woods behind Leah's house? There's a trail through the trees that's much more interesting."

"You're the guide," he said, inclining his bare head, snowflakes twinkling in his dark blond hair.

A few minutes later, after they crossed the road and passed Leah's former home, they followed the meandering creek that eventually fed the Brazos River and was bordered by canebrake thickets. Past a grove of dormant pecan trees, they cantered along a narrow path bordered by bare cottonwoods whose branches scraped together like bony fingers in wind that surged and abated.

When they had slowed to a trot, Jared looked over at Sue. She rode with natural grace, and his eyes roamed over her, passion once again rising in him. The woods were silent, exquisitely primeval, as if no human had ever invaded the sweet quiet. Despite the near-mystical calm, they talked and didn't disturb the tranquillity of the forest. It was a time of getting to know each other, and the time passed swiftly.

"Interesting," he said at last. "We seem to have a lot in common."

"Yes. I guess we—" Her words broke off with a small startled cry when a squirrel darted out of the brambles in front of Teeny-Bop and the mare reared back on her hind legs, spilling Sue out of the saddle before she had time to react.

"Damn!" she shouted, jarred as she landed smack on her buttocks in the few inches of snow.

Only her dignity was injured, however, and she wasted no time picking herself up and dusting herself off even as Jared dismounted and lightly grasped her shoulders. His hands moved down her arms to span her waist.

"You okay?" he questioned, his tone urgent, his low-timbred voice deepening. "Are you hurt?"

"Just my pride."

His gray eyes captured hers and darkened with smoky intensity.

"Susan," he whispered as he pulled her to him and his mouth covered hers.

His lips, firm yet tender, parted hers, and as he pushed the tip of his tongue into her mouth, a jolt ran like raw uninsulated current through her whole body. Breathless, her heart thudding frantically, she kissed him because she wanted to, needed to. But as his kiss deepened, inbred caution flashed through her brain and she struggled to overcome her desire for physical pleasure with common sense. Succeeding after several delightful but confusing seconds, she pulled away from Jared, shaking her head.

"I think we'd better go back now."

"Why?" he asked, his voice appealingly husky as he lifted her chin with one finger to make her look him in the eye. "We both enjoyed it, Susan. We're going to enjoy it again."

Once more his warm mouth took possession of hers, making her dizzy until she again sought control, reluctantly dragging her lips from his and taking a jerky step out of his embrace.

"Why?" he repeated, passion glinting in his eyes. "Another man in your life? Somebody back in Atlanta?"

"Nobody special, no," she murmured. "It's nothing like that. It's just that I think we should head back to the ranch."

She shouldn't be rushed. She was special. Those thoughts ran through his mind as he reined in desire and finally nodded. "All right, we'll go back. You look

58

cold; your nose is getting red. Besides, I have to admit the top of my head's freezing without a hat. Guess my hair's beginning to get thin."

Sue grinned.

CHAPTER FOUR

That night Sue drove Jared and Tommy across the road again. At the door Jared asked her in. "One of my friends gave me a bottle of Scotch for Christmas. Come in and we'll open it," he suggested softly over his sleeping son's head. "It's a chilly night. A drink will warm us up."

Accepting his invitation, she walked ahead of them through the kitchen to the hall, where she switched on the light so he could see up the stairs. As Jared started past her, Tommy shifted in his arms. A well-worn orange blanket covered with fading yet still jolly fat green frogs fell to the floor at her feet.

"Looks like it's been cuddled a lot," she commented, picking up the blanket to tuck it securely in the crook of Jared's right arm. "Is it his security?"

"Yes, and it's priceless. He won't sleep without it, and I'd hate to think what would happen if he ever lost it."

She smiled reminiscently. "I had a security blanket, too, hung on to it for years. Jace used to tease me about it all the time. He hid it once and wouldn't tell me where it was. So I got his air rifle and threatened to shoot him. Mama put a stop to that real fast. Big brothers can be a pain sometimes."

"So my little brother has told me," Jared murmured, giving her a devilish smile. "I don't know why he feels that way, though. I never ever did anything to aggravate him when we were kids."

"Of course not," she replied glibly, looking up in frank disbelief.

Jared started up the stairs. "Just let me get Tommy tucked in and I'll be right down."

Nodding, she wandered into the parlor and turned on a lamp. It was a warm, comfortable room. Leah had chosen just the right decor for it, homey yet not the least bit dull. Sitting on the royal blue sofa, Sue listened to Jared's quiet footsteps as he ran lightly back down the stairs, then strode into the parlor carrying a bottle of Chivas Regal.

"Aaron drove us to the airport, then gave me this," he told Sue, going to the small liquor cabinet on the far side of the room and taking out two cut-glass tumblers. "I really don't want to have to take it back home on the plane, so you're going to have to help me drink it."

"I hope that doesn't mean you want us to polish off the whole bottle tonight."

Jared chuckled. "No, I don't think Leah and Jace would be too pleased if you got back to the ranch smashed. And you'd be even less pleased tomorrow morning when you woke up with a whopping hangover."

"You're right. I can certainly do without that."

"Scotch and water all right for you?"

"Fine."

"Ice?"

"Definitely. And light on the Scotch."

Nodding, Jared carried the glasses and bottle out to the kitchen, then returned a couple of minutes later to hand her one drink and sit down next to her. Ice tinkled against the crystal as he touched the rim of his tumbler to hers, proposing a toast. "To Texas."

"No born-and-bred Texan could refuse to drink to that," she said, taking a small sip. "I want to make a toast too. To Tommy and you—I hope you have a very merry Christmas here and I hope he won't miss his grandparents too much."

Jared's smoky eyes darkened as he regarded her intently. "I get the feeling you like that kid of mine."

"Of course I do, and I want him to be happy while he's here."

"Then you don't have to worry. He's in seventh heaven. All the hands call him little cowpoke; Cookie loves having him around, and Zeke thrills him with those tall tales. You've made a difference too," Jared added, his deep voice lowering. "He tried not to like you, but it looks like he's fighting a losing battle. I noticed at dinner tonight that he sat beside you at the table and even showed you the Matchbox car he had in his pocket. I have to hand it to you; your strategy's working. How did you know it would be best to let him make the moves toward you?"

"I'm the old schoolmarm, remember? I've had to deal with suspicious children before. They're not like the shy ones. Shy kids need to be courted with obvious affection. The ones like Tommy hate being treated like that. With them, you have to be cagey. Polite and accessible, but never too chummy too fast. Being aloof makes them start wondering about you, about why you don't try quite as hard as other adults to get through to them. Most kids can't resist a mystery, so they start approaching you to find out what makes you different."

"It's an intriguing strategy."

"Unfortunately, it doesn't work all the time."

"But it is working with Tommy. You're the first young woman he's shown signs of liking in a very long time."

"But he's in school now. What about his teacher?"

"She's in her fifties and he loves her; says she's like Grandma."

But there must be some young women in your life he has to relate to?"

Jared shook his head. "Oh, I go out often enough— I'm not a monk, after all—but I don't see anybody on a regular basis."

"Ah-ha." Sue grinned. "A regular playboy, huh?"

"You bet. The swinging divorcé," he said. "Do you know what a businessman's life can be like? Late nights at the office, long meetings, taking home piles of work only to find another stack the next day. There are nights when I don't get more than three or four hours' sleep. I don't always feel up to pursuing a dynamite social life."

"Sounds a little like teaching school. Up half the night grading papers and planning lessons for the next day. I'm lucky if I have time to say hello to my neighbors sometimes."

"Guess we're both a couple of sticks-in-the-mud, aren't we?"

She laughed merrily. "It's beginning to sound that way."

"Actually I don't want to be a workaholic."

"Me either."

"But sometimes it's easier to keep busy than to think."

"I guess," Sue conceded, pensively nibbling her lower lip. "But when we do that, we're just trying to escape reality, aren't we? And that never succeeds indefinitely. We have to face up to facts, unpleasant as they may be."

"Tell me. What unpleasant facts have you had to face?"

"Mama dying," she said, and added, "Then Daddy dying so soon after. Once in a while it hits me that they're both gone . . . I'm not sure I've ever accepted that deep down inside."

His heart went out to her. Despite her outward bravery, she hurt in her soul. Although both his parents were still living, Jared could imagine the loss she felt, and he took her glass from her hand to put it down with his on the coffee table. Cupping her face in his palms, he stroked the line of her jaw. "I didn't mean to dredge up painful memories."

"You didn't," she murmured, her faint smile resigned. "There are some sorrows that never really go away, and the least little thing can bring them to mind again. It's not your fault."

"Susan," he whispered, wanting to hold her close.

Before she could react, he slipped his arms around her, drawing her nearer. Her breath caught in her throat as he lowered his head and his lips took bold possession of hers.

She couldn't resist him. His warmth, his strength, the potent aura of virility that clung to him like a second skin made her senses swim. She succumbed to his tender aggression, her heart pounding in her ears, every inch of her skin becoming sensitized as her mouth flowered open beneath the compelling pressure of his, and his tongue entered.

With the tip of her tongue she parried the tender thrust of his, then drew it in deeper as his powerful arms tightened around her. She wound hers up around his neck, her fingers tangling in the thick sandy hair grazing his nape. Wild heat rampaged through her, weakening her knees when he lifted her closer still until she was half reclining across his hard thighs. His breath tasted like Scotch as he kissed her. Their lips met, clung, parted again and again as his breathing became as quick and troubled as hers; she could feel the rapid thudding of his heart.

"Beautiful Susan," he murmured, nibbling the lobe of her right ear with his teeth. "Susan, you're delicious." The tip of his tongue teased the corners of her mouth, sending cascading shivers down the length of her spine.

Pressing closer, she glided her hands across his shoulders. And when he suddenly released her to rake his fingers through his hair, she looked at him, her eyes widening with surprise. "What's—"

"This is crazy. I didn't plan to let this happen. I wanted it to because I'm attracted to you, but now that I've gotten to know you better, I realize you'd never want to be involved in a casual relationship," he tried to explain. "And in two weeks you'll be back in Atlanta and I'll be back in New York."

Smiling wryly, she caressed his collarbone at the open neck of his shirt. "Haven't you ever heard of that new invention, the airplane? It makes travel much faster, and it's not all that far from New York to Atlanta."

"Susan . . ."

"Kiss me again," she softly commanded, slipping her arms around him.

He pulled her tightly against him again, his firm lips brushing slowly back and forth over the parted softness of hers.

The tender yet potent persuasion of his mouth and the feel of his large hands coursing like fire over her back created waves of excitement that rushed through her body. Arching against him, Sue moaned softly when he pulled her blouse free from beneath the waistband of her skirt and his fingers slipped under her silky camisole to graze over her breasts. Through the sheer lace cups of her bra, his caresses seared, kindling wildfires on her skin.

"Oh, Jared," she murmured as he cupped the weight of her breasts in his palms and his thumbs stroked upward to play over their heated peaks, tantalizing until they swelled beneath his fingers.

Her heart thundering, Sue unbuttoned his shirt to run her hands over his warm, hair-roughened chest. He felt so good, so wonderfully desirable. Tentatively she played with his flat nipples, drawing slow circles around them.

Need burned through his bloodstream to gather in throbbing force in his center. Winding the thick swath of her silken hair around one hand, he tilted her head back, nibbled her creamy neck with his teeth, and licked the fluttering pulse in her throat with the tip of his tongue. He was close to losing control when she said softly in his ear, "Right? New York and Atlanta aren't that far apart, are they?"

Remembering his good intentions, he gave a low groan and once again let her go. "The distance isn't the problem, Sue. I'm trying to tell you that I don't want to get involved in a serious relationship, but I doubt you'd be interested in a two-week fling."

Quick resentment flashed in her eyes. "It would have been nice of you to tell me that before I threw myself at you."

"You didn't throw yourself at me," he said quietly, reaching for her hand, then shaking his head apologetically when she wouldn't allow him to take it. "I enjoyed what we just shared. I'm only trying to be honest with you."

"Well, give yourself a pat on the back, because you're succeeding," she muttered, hastily stuffing her blouse back into her skirt. "You're honest, all right, to the point of being blunt." She rose to her feet. "Good night, Mr. Ryder."

He stood also, blocking her path and gently grasping her shoulders. "I just didn't want to deceive you. And I have the feeling casual affairs aren't for you."

"Oh, you're very perceptive. Now that we understand each other perfectly, I'll—"

"Susan, please. I know I botched this," he interrupted. "But can't we at least be friends?"

"I'll think about it," she answered. Shrugging his

hands from her shoulders, she walked around him and left the house.

The next morning three inches of snow covered the ground. Jared went with Jace and the hands out on the range, leaving Tommy in the den playing demolition derby with his small cars, providing his own grinding sound effects. Deciding both she and Teeny-Bop needed exercise, Sue went out for a ride. When she returned to the barnyard an hour later, Tommy came out of the house bundled up warmly in his coat and a knit hat. Wisps of his fine pale gold hair stuck out from under it, and as he pushed the fringe feathering his brow aside, he looked up, saw Sue, and stopped in his tracks, his eyes glued on her horse.

Judging by the appreciative glow in his eyes, Sue was sure Teeny-Bop had made a conquest. Stroking the mare's silky mane, she gave the boy a small smile. "Good morning, Tommy."

He stepped closer. "Hi. He's a nice horse. What's his name?"

"He's a she. Her name's Teeny-Bop."

Tommy laughed. "That's a silly name."

"It is a funny one," she admitted, chuckling with him. "But I wanted to name her that because when I was a teenager, my Daddy used to call me Teeny-Bop."

"Doesn't he call you that anymore?"

"No, I'm afraid not. He died, Tommy."

The child's face grew solemn. "That's sad. My granddaddy's dog died in the summer. I felt bad. I liked Seymour a lot."

"I'm sorry. I know you must miss him."

68

"Yeah. But Daddy told me Seymour was real old."

Sue nodded sympathetically. "Well, I know you wouldn't have wanted him to live if he felt bad."

"That's what Daddy told me," the boy murmured, then asked quite naturally, "Was your Daddy real old, too?"

"Not too old. But he felt bad, so I think it's probably better that he just went to sleep and didn't wake up, even though Jace and I were very sad about it."

"Your mother too?"

"My mother died three years before Dad."

"Oh." Something akin to a closed expression settled on Tommy's face. "I don't have a mother either."

Compassion squeezing her heart, Sue said nothing. So that was the way he looked at his situation, she thought. His mother didn't care enough about him even to visit him, therefore he didn't have a mother. It was a shame he had to feel that way, but his reasoning was logical for a child.

"Is Teeny-Bop a nice horse?" Tommy inquired, interrupting Sue's reverie. "Can I pet her?"

"Oh, sure, she's very gentle. Come over here and stroke her nose. She likes that."

As the little boy rubbed the mare's nose, then flashed Sue a grin that warmed her like an unexpected ray of sunshine, she asked, "Would you like to ride her?"

His eyes said yes but a small frown expressed uncertainty. "She's awful big. I don't wanna fall off."

"I guess a pony would be more your size, but you can ride her with me, if you want to. How about it?"

Tommy hesitated only a second before nodding. "Okay."

Pleased, hoping she was making a breakthrough, Sue told him to come around to her left side, leaned down in the saddle, and placed her hands beneath his arms. She groaned, pretending to have great difficulty lifting him. "You're going to have to help. Give a little jump while I pick you up so I can get you up here with me. I didn't know you were such a big, sturdy boy. I bet you're going to grow up to be as tall as your dad. Maybe taller."

It was the perfect thing to say. Tommy beamed with delight and boosted himself up as she lifted him into the saddle in front of her. Giving him the reins, she placed her hands over his. "Now, just relax. If you want Teeny-Bop to go toward the house, just tug a little on this rein. If you want to go—"

"I know how to do it," he proudly set her straight. "My daddy lets me ride with him a lot. And next summer I'm gonna ride all by myself."

Duly chastised, Sue smiled to herself and gave Teeny-Bop a quiet command. With Tommy controlling the reins, they rode in circles around the barnyard.

"Too slow," he complained after several walking laps. "I wanna go faster."

"Okay. We'll canter down the driveway and back," Sue agreed. "But I have to hold on." Putting her arms around him, hoping he wouldn't tense up and grateful when he didn't, she grasped the pommel with both hands while gently tapping her heels against the mare's flanks. "Okay, cowpoke, head down the drive."

70

After three round-trips, Tommy's chubby cheeks were flushed with both cold and excitement. "Time to head back to the barn," Sue told him on the last lap. "We don't want you to get too chilly."

"Aww, I'm not cold."

"Not yet, maybe. But what about Teeny-Bop? I think she might be ready to get back to her warm stall. And we want to take good care of her, don't we?"

The appeal to his natural love for animals worked like a charm, and she had no trouble enlisting his help in removing Teeny-Bop's bridle and saddle, then grooming her. Those tasks accomplished, Sue asked Tommy to give the horse two scoops of oats from a nearby bin. Bending her sleek head, the mare began munching contentedly.

"She's making me hungry," Sue commented casually. "How about you? Why don't we go have some of those oatmeal cookies Leah baked yesterday? And some hot chocolate too. Do you like hot chocolate?"

"Mmm," Tommy replied, "I like it lots."

She was definitely making progress with him. He was no longer afraid to be friendly, and she felt good as they walked back to the house together.

Leah was in the shower, so Sue and Tommy had the kitchen all to themselves. After she heated milk, she added a generous amount of chocolate syrup to it, then poured it into two cups. Topping both with miniature marshmallows, she put a plateful of cookies on the table and sat down across from the small boy, who quickly reached out to grab three of them at one time.

Sue ate two, her gaze going to him whenever he

wasn't looking. He was a sweet little boy and she knew her affection for him was growing. But it was too soon to show him that, and when he took another cookie, she shrugged indifferently. "I hope that doesn't spoil your lunch. Don't blame me if your dad asks you why you're not hungry."

"I'll be hungry," he said between bites. "It's fun to eat."

She smiled. "Do you think stories are fun too? I'll tell you one if you'd like to hear it."

He nodded.

"Okay," she began. "There's a place called Connecticut and a boy named Tommy visits his grandparents' farm there. Tommy has a big beautiful horse named Black Satin. Black Satin's the fastest, strongest horse in the whole world and he loves Tommy. Together they go on exciting adventures. You may find this hard to believe, but one day they found a pretty girl lost in the woods. She was crying and they . . ."

Twenty minutes later Jared opened the back door and walked into the warm kitchen to find his son smiling happily at Sue and bobbing his head up and down as he proclaimed, "Oh, I liked that story! Tell me another one about Tommy and Black Satin."

"But I can't tell you about all their adventures in one day," she said, smiling back at the young boy, then glancing over her shoulder at his father. "Besides, your dad's back and from the looks of him, he could use some hot chocolate too. Or coffee."

"Coffee, please," Jared requested, then listened as Tommy babbled a quick synopsis of the story Sue had told him. He smiled. "This boy Tommy sounds a lot like you."

"He is like me. He even goes to see his granddaddy and grandma on a farm in Conne'cut. Just like I do! Sue tells real good stories. When will you tell me another one, Sue?"

"Soon," she said, giving him a warm smile. "I promise."

"Right now, my man, you'd better go wash the cookie crumbs off your face," Jared suggested, lifting his son and swinging him around once before shooing him out of the kitchen.

Left alone with Jared, Sue poured a cup of coffee for him, her heart seeming to do silly little flips as she glanced over her shoulder and found him watching her every move. Reliving last night's embarrassment, she took a deep, steadying breath. "Well, how did you like cowpoking today?"

"I'm still a greenhorn, I guess." He chuckled. "As you see, I came back before the others. That wind whips right through you."

"Oh, but you're used to weather worse than this. I have a feeling you came back early to check on Tommy."

"True," he conceded. "But it's still colder than a well-digger's— Never mind. It's just cold out there."

Sue put the cup of coffee on the table as he took a chair, but before she could sit down with him, he reached out with his hand to catch hold of her wrist. When he tried to pull her down on his lap, she resisted, her lips tightening. "No way, buster. Maybe we can be friends, but after what happened last night, friendship's all you'd better expect from me."

His gray eyes held hers. "I did a lot of thinking after you left, Susan, and I've changed my mind. I had a lousy marriage, but that doesn't mean I should avoid a serious involvement when I meet a very special woman like you."

She was suddenly breathless. "Meaning you're interested in more than a two-week fling?"

"Yes, I think we could have much more than that together."

"Do you think I'm special because I've been able to get Tommy to like me a little?"

"More than a little. I think you've won him over."

"Don't count your chickens."

"Whatever; you know it's not because of Tommy I want you."

"How can I be sure?"

"Trust me."

All at once she did, and she made no further efforts to resist. When she sat down on his lap, his strong arms swiftly embraced her and his warm mouth covered hers.

She gasped with pleasure, and her lips parted. His deepening kiss thrilled her. Exquisite tingles danced over the surface of her skin, awakening every nerve ending. His tongue played teasingly over hers, and she kissed him back until his powerful hands wandered up from her waist to sweep over her breasts, then rest there, his lean fingers stroking, caressing. He made her want him so much, and the fact that she liked and respected him intensified her need to be closer to him—as close as possible.

It was only when she heard Tommy singing down the hall that she realized that they were sitting in the kitchen, where someone might walk in at any moment. A private person, she didn't want them to have to share their feelings for each other—not yet, anyway. She pulled away from him, shaking her head.

"Enough."

"Not nearly enough."

"But Tommy and Leah are just down the hall."

"True, but you're irresistible, woman. God knows I tried to resist. But last night I realized I was fighting a losing battle."

She giggled as he nibbled at her chin. "Stop that."

"Can't. You taste too good for me to quit."

"I never imagined you could be so playful."

"I'm not always serious. Sometimes I can be a real fun-loving fellow."

Laughing, she slipped off his lap, then had to lightly swat his hands when he reached for her once more. She skipped out of his reach and shook an admonishing finger at him. "If you don't behave—"

Tommy darted into the kitchen before she could finish what she'd started to say. When he began to beg her for another story, she looked at Jared over the top of his head, a soft glow of happiness filling her eyes. Both Jared and Tommy had become part of her life so quickly. It was good to know she was also becoming important to them.

CHAPTER FIVE

Friday afternoon Sue and Jared went to Fort Worth for some last minute Christmas shopping. Tommy had seemed to realize his father was probably going to buy something for him and hadn't kicked up a fuss about going along. He'd even promised to take his nap promptly at two o'clock and obey Leah faithfully while they were gone.

Talking easily, Jared and Sue made the drive seem short for each other, and as she drove her car into a vacant parking space, they smiled. "I love going shopping during the last few days before Christmas," she told him. "It's so exciting."

"And hectic."

"That too. But there's something in the air, something special most people seem to share, don't you think?"

"I think you're a romantic," he answered as they got out of the car, "but you're right, it's exhilarating."

"Exactly," she murmured, taking the arm he offered as they stepped up on the curb.

In the city all the snow had melted, but drafts of icy wind funneled along the wide boulevards, making the festive yuletide decorations strung along the thoroughfares dance and bob. As Sue and Jared turned a corner, a strong gust lifted her hair off her shoulders to stream out behind her in silky disarray.

"It's unusually cold here this winter," she said, turning up the collar of her coat. "But I guess it seems pretty mild to you compared to winter in New York."

"I've been colder. But then, I've been warmer, too, even in New York during the winter. Have you ever been there?"

"A couple of times in the summer."

"The city's beautiful when we get a heavy snow—at least right after it's fallen and hasn't turned to slush. Everything seems to glimmer, and there's a hushed quiet. I think you'd like it there when it snows."

"It does sound lovely," she agreed, stopping at the next corner to incline her head toward the store across the street. "There's *the* place to shop in this part of the world. Want to go in?"

He grimaced comically. "It may be the fashionable place to go, but it's also expensive. Maybe my wallet would be better off if we went to some other store."

"Oh, thank goodness you said that," Sue gave a theatrical sigh of relief, her eyes twinkling merrily. "I thought you might want to go in, but if you had, I couldn't have done anything but browse. The prices are too high for me too. Someday, when I'm incredibly wealthy, I might sweep regally in there and buy

77

whatever catches my fancy. I shall be quite elegant and blasé about the whole thing, I assure you."

Laughing together as she haughtily tossed her head, they crossed over to the next block, where they threaded their way among shoppers bearing packages until they pushed open the doors to enter a very nice but less expensive department store. A rush of warmth welcomed them, making Sue's chilled cheeks tingle. Piped-in holiday music floated over the hustle and bustle in the aisles.

For a few seconds Sue hummed along. Then she smiled up at Jared. "See, even the music makes it exciting."

"It also encourages you to buy more."

"Cynic."

"Realist."

"Well, maybe so, but I'm still swept up in the holiday spirit. And so are you, whether you'll admit it or not."

"Oh, I'm not ashamed to admit it," he said, quickly moving her out of the path of a frenzied shopper bearing an armload of gaily wrapped parcels. As he sped past them, the one teetering on the top of his load slid off and hit the floor.

Picking it up, Jared placed it more securely on the pile.

"Thank you kindly," the harried man said, sadly shaking his head. "Every year I tell myself I'm going to shop early but I never do it. Guess I'm never gonna learn. Thanks again."

He was off again, making a beeline toward the perfume counter as Sue and Jared exchanged amused smiles.

"Thank goodness I've already bought most of the presents I want to give," she said. "I'd hate to be in his shoes. There are only a couple more gifts I have to get. How about you?"

"I just have to buy two or three things too," Jared answered. "After I decided to bring Tommy down here for the holidays, I mailed everything he'd put on his list to Leah. But you know kids. He keeps adding little items, so I'm still not finished. I have to go to the toy department. Know where that is?"

"This way." She directed him to the up escalator. Borne upward to the second floor, she nodded to the right. "Toys and Games. Can I help you find something?"

"You sure can. Tommy wants a cowboy outfit, although I can't imagine why."

"Me either," she said, chuckling. "Couldn't have anything to do with Zeke and his tall tales, could it?"

"How'd you guess?"

"Just naturally bright. But I'm glad we came up here. I want to give Tommy something too. Got any suggestions?"

"Let me think about it," was Jared's answer as they walked up one aisle and down another, at last locating the section where boxes of children's costumes were stacked. After a short search he found a cowboy suit in his son's size that included a Western shirt, fringed vest, and trousers with simulated leather chaps. For a costume the quality of fabric was adequate, but the hat with it was a disgrace. Sue winced the minute she saw it.

"That thing looks like you could run a broom straw through it," she said. But her expression immediately brightened. "But I tell you what: you leave that out and I'll go to the children's clothing department and get him a hat he'll love. That'll be my gift to him."

"You're talking money now," Jared said softly, shaking his head. "I know you like Tommy, but you're going to have to pay a lot for an authentic cowboy hat."

"I'm not complaining, so don't you worry about it. If I didn't want to buy him something nice, I wouldn't. All right?"

After a moment he nodded, one corner of his mouth curving up. "Whatever you say. I might as well agree with you, since I know how strong-willed you are. You're going to do what you want to no matter what I say."

"We're making progress," she said. "You *are* beginning to understand me."

Together they waited for a clerk to ring up Jared's purchase. After he paid with cash, they walked back toward the escalator, where she inquired, "Okay, where do you want to go now?"

"The women's department. I brought a gift for Leah and Jace, but I'd like to get something just for her, too, since she is my favorite cousin."

Back on the first floor several moments later, Sue pointed him in the right direction, told him she was going to the children's clothing department, and agreed to meet him at the shoe department in a half-hour.

But she made a quick detour on the way to her destination. Wandering into the section containing menswear and accessories, she quickly browsed and found a gift for Jared. After purchasing the gold-filled

80

pen and pencil set, she hurried to the back of the store, where she found a cowboy hat for Tommy, one that looked much better than the one included with the costume. Jared had been right; it was relatively expensive, but she smiled as she gladly paid the clerk. Tommy was a precious child.

Her shopping done, she found Jared waiting for her in front of a shoe display. Seeing her walking toward him, he smiled. That was all it took to make her heart beat faster, and she had to take a shaky breath as she smiled back at him.

"There's a coffee shop just down the block," she said as they left the store. "Buy you a cup?"

"Sounds good."

Even in the small restaurant, soft Christmas music was being played, and as they settled into a back booth, Sue tilted her head to one side. "What is that carol? I can't think of the name of it but I remember it from Christmas pageants we had in school when I was a kid. Do you know it?"

"Sorry," he said after ordering two coffees from a waitress. "Of course it's been a long time since I was in a school pageant or even went to one."

"That'll change soon. Now that Tommy's in grammar school, you'll be seeing lots of plays."

"Is that a warning?" he asked, smiling his thanks to the waitress as she returned with their coffee. "Now that you've jogged my memory, I recall some school productions I was in that were real bombs."

"But that's part of the fun. Besides, when it's Tommy up on that stage, you'll think the production's good enough to hit Broadway. And he'll love it. At school I'm usually backstage during pageants and

81

plays, and the kids are always so excited. Nothing thrills them more than putting on costumes."

Stirring his coffee, he looked at her for a long moment. "You really love kids, don't you?"

"Sure. I'd be in the wrong profession if I didn't. But you like them, too, don't you?"

"I'm not around many. But I like *my* kid."

"Do you think you'd want to have another child someday?"

Holding back a grin, he waggled his eyebrows at her. "If this is a proposition, keep talking. I'm interested."

"Oh, be serious. I just wondered if you wanted—"

"Yes. I believe I would like to have more children sometime."

"That's all I wanted: a simple answer." Glancing down at his packages on the tabletop, she reached for one. "Oh, let me see what you bought Leah."

He playfully smacked her hand away, shaking his head. "Don't be nosy."

"You bought me a present too?" It was a rhetorical question; she already knew the answer and pretended to be dismayed. "Oh, you shouldn't have, I mean I . . ." She started to get up. "I, uh . . . just remembered I forgot something. Why don't you finish your coffee? I have to run back to the store for just a second. Excuse me."

"Sit down," he commanded, capturing her wrist. "Maybe I got you a gift; maybe I didn't. But even if you think I did, you don't have to run out and buy me one."

"Oh. Okay, if that's the way you feel about it," she

said flatly but couldn't help laughing, spoiling her little act.

"Hmm, two can play this game," he murmured, grabbing the department store bag beside her navy purse. "I think I'll just have a look in here and see what—"

"Give me that!" she protested, still laughing as she reached across the table. "Jared, don't you dare open it!"

"Careful. You'll spill your coffee."

Snatching the bag out of his hand, she sat back. "Now who's being nosy?"

"I am. What did you get me?"

"Nothing."

"Aw, come on, just give me a hint."

"Devil."

When Sue drove Jared and Tommy across the road that evening, she didn't plan to stay, but Jared had other ideas. "Come in for a while," he invited. "Keep me company."

"I don't know. It's sort of late. I should—"

"Come in and have a drink. After all, you're supposed to be helping me finish that bottle of Scotch."

"Well, yes, but not tonight. I should be getting back to the ranch."

"What's the matter? Are you afraid to be alone with me?"

"No," she lied, shaking her head vehemently. "It's not that."

"What is it then?" Shifting Tommy in his arms, he lowered his voice further still as his son's eyes opened

83

briefly, then fluttered shut again. "Why won't you come in, Susan? Do I bore you?"

"You know better than that."

"Well, then, I can only assume I make you nervous."

"Why should you? You're not an ogre."

"Well, then, come in and stay awhile."

She threw up her hands, knowing if she left now it would look like she was running away from him, and he might realize her feelings for him were growing stronger as they spent more time together. And she wasn't at all sure she wanted him to realize that. "All right, I'll stay a little while," she said, stepping inside the house. "A drink would be nice."

After tucking Tommy into bed, Jared tiptoed out of the room and down the hall. Reaching the bottom of the stairs, he went directly into the kitchen to make two drinks, then carried them to the parlor, where he paused in the doorway to watch Susan. Her back to him, she was looking at the Christmas tree he had bought that afternoon as they had headed home. Leah had provided plenty of decorations she hadn't needed for the tree in the ranch house, and he and Tommy had trimmed the tree before dinner. He wanted his son to wake up Christmas morning and run downstairs to find his presents instead of having to walk across the road, which would have taken much of the magic out of the whole thing.

While he'd been putting Tommy to bed, Susan had plugged in the lights. Soft ambers, blues, and reds glowed among the rich green branches and highlighted her chestnut hair, which tumbled in light waves down around her shoulders. A vision came to mind of how she might look after a night of passionate lovemaking, her thick hair tousled and framing her lovely face, her eyes a deep blue, her features relaxed and content. He wanted to see her that way, needed to, and that need was more than physical.

Something instinctive told her she was being watched, and she quickly turned around, smiling faintly as Jared walked over to her to hand her one of the glasses he carried.

Murmuring her thanks, she ignored the sudden erratic beating of her pulse and turned her attention back to the tree. "You guys did a great job. It's beautiful."

"I think so, even if Tommy did bunch up most of the ornaments and icicles on the right side."

"That gives it its own identity. Sometimes perfection can be boring."

"Ah, that's a relief," Jared said wryly, motioning her toward the sofa. "Now I know I must not bore you, because I'm far from perfect."

"Oh, drat, I thought you were," she countered, managing not to choke on a sip of her drink when he switched off the lamp, leaving only the tree lights to illuminate the room. "What a disappointment. But now that you've told me the truth, you might as well tell me what's not perfect about you."

"For one thing, I sometimes snore."

"Oh, no!" She slapped one hand against her cheek. "How horrible! Is there any other terrible defect you should tell me about?"

"I think I mentioned this before," he said, dropping his head sadly in pretense. "My hair may be getting thinner on top."

"You *are* a wreck," she teased. "Any other faults, Mr. Ryder?"

Without warning his jaw hardened as his expression sobered and he looked directly into her eyes once again. "As a matter of fact, I have to admit I can be a lousy judge of character once in a while."

Sue understood what he meant instantly, but her gaze never wavered from his. "I have a feeling you're talking about your ex-wife," she murmured. "Am I right?"

"On the button. I had her pegged wrong from the beginning." After taking a swallow of the amber liquid in his glass, he shook his head, his features gentling slightly. "I'm not saying it was all her fault that our marriage didn't work. It wasn't. I should have known better than to marry her, but at the time we seemed to have more in common than we really did." With one fingertip he toyed with the ice floating in his drink. "Tommy was an accident—one I certainly don't regret. But even before he was born, we were having problems. Somehow we stayed together for three years after he was born. It didn't surprise me when she walked out, but I couldn't believe she could leave her own son and never look back, never even ask to see him."

"She may be very sorry she did someday," Sue offered. "How do you think he'd react if she changed her mind and tried to get involved in his life again?"

"I hope to hell she doesn't even think about it," he muttered. "She's done enough harm already. I can't forget how often he asked where she was right after she left. I thought about lying and saying she had died, but I knew he'd find out what really happened

86

sooner or later and maybe hate me for not telling him the truth. So I just told him she didn't want to live with us anymore. She'd never been a great mother, but she was the only one he had. He cried for days, and after he stopped he started shying away from all young women. I can't say I blame him."

With tears building behind her eyes, Sue put her glass down and touched Jared's cheek with light fingertips as she huskily whispered, "I'm so sorry. But don't be offended. I'm not pitying you. I'm just sorry it all worked out the way it did. Okay? You're not going to snap at me again, are you?"

"No." A semblance of a smile moved his carved lips as he too put his drink aside, took her comforting hand in both of his, and raised it to his mouth to kiss each slender finger.

She trembled as a plunging desire shot through her and her breath caught. She knew in her heart she had fallen in love with him.

He felt her quiver and pulled her to him, his arms tightly embracing her shapely body, his fingers in her faintly scented hair tilting her head back, his mouth swiftly possessing hers, opening it for his pleasure and hers.

Sue wrapped her arms around his waist, arching against him, her tongue moving in an erotic dance with his. She was soon lost in a blossoming emotion intensified by the sexual delight he ignited with his plundering kisses and exploring caresses. When he lowered her onto the sofa, she didn't resist. He kissed her again and again, devouring the sweetness of her mouth, and she kissed him back, hungry for the taste of him.

His heart thudded as fast as a jackhammer in his chest as passion surged through his bloodstream, gathering force. "Susan." He groaned softly when she pressed harder against him, her fingers drifting like a light breeze through his hair. "I want you so much, honey."

And she wanted him, ached to be nearer, longed for intimacy. When he raised up just enough to open her pale yellow blouse, take it off, and then unfasten the single front hook of her bra, she held her breath, waiting for his touch.

"Beautiful," he murmured hoarsely, looking down at her, then caressing her breasts, his gray eyes dark and gleaming. With gentle demand he drew his fingertips upward in slow circles until he found her rosy nipples, which he tenderly fondled between his thumbs and forefingers until they swelled with arousal.

"Jared," she whispered, her hands wandering feverishly over his broad back. And she moaned with exquisite delight as he feathered the tip of his tongue over one nipple, then drew it deeply into his mouth, pulling on it with slowly graduating pressure.

She wanted to give herself and take back all he could give in return, but when he unsnapped the waistband of her jeans and began slowly lowering the zipper a few minutes later, she tensed once again. She couldn't help it. She wanted him, yes, but she had just realized she loved him and that in itself was traumatic enough; never in her wildest dreams had she imagined she'd ever fall in love with a man in less than a week, but she had. She had to cope with that fact first before she could explore an intimate relationship with him. And although she still ached for the physical satisfaction only he could give, she pulled away from him.

"I—I'm not ready for this," she said, her voice shaky as she rose to her feet. "Everything's happening too fast, Jared. It's too soon."

"Susan," he said huskily, "wait. Don't go yet."

But she didn't dare hesitate. She rebuttoned her shirt and picked up her jacket.

"All right, I'll let you go—for now," he murmured, his slow smile both understanding and indulgent. But he drew her into his arms again. "Just promise me you'll think about this when you go to sleep tonight."

When he kissed her with possessive insistence, she kissed him back, feeling dizzy.

"Stop it! Stop it!" a small, shrill voice suddenly demanded, startling them and making them jump away from each other to jerk their heads toward the doorway. Tommy stood there, his cheeks red with anger.

"Stop it!" he wailed one more time.

Frightened, Sue started toward him, but Jared's hand shot out to stop her as Tommy spun around and ran up the stairs.

"Maybe you'd better stay here," he said, a worried frown creasing his forehead. "I'll go see what's wrong."

For the following five minutes Sue paced the parlor, wondering what was happening upstairs. Tommy had looked so upset, and she had no idea why. A nightmare? Perhaps. Maybe he had been half asleep when he came down. Finally Jared returned, concern written all over his lean face, and she hurried to him to ask, "Is he okay?"

"He's calmed down a little. But he won't tell me what upset him."

"Maybe a bad dream?"

"Maybe, but I just don't know." Jared massaged his temples. "Or maybe it bothered him to see us kissing —it's something new to him. I go out sometimes, but I've never brought a woman home with me."

"Oh."

"I guess we'd better be a little more discreet."

"Yes, I guess so," Sue agreed. "But I really thought he was beginning to care about me."

"He does care."

"Then why . . ."

"You work with children; you know they're not always easy to read. But we'll work this out. Maybe Tommy did just have a bad dream."

"I'd like to believe that, but now that you mention it . . ." Her words trailed off, and with a shrug she headed out of the parlor. "I'll see you tomorrow, Jared."

"Good night, Susan," he murmured, then walked her to the side door, watching as she got into the car and headed back across the road.

CHAPTER SIX

On Christmas Eve Tommy was too excited to sit still. By nine o'clock he was yawning, yet continually jumping up to look out the window in the ranch house den. He always came back to climb up beside his father on the sofa, but once there, he did nothing except wiggle.

"It's past your bedtime, sport," Jared finally said. "Hopefully your blanket will calm you down a little. Come on, I'll tuck you in."

The child balked, shaking his head. "Don't wanna go to sleep yet."

"Maybe not, but you have to," Jared said firmly, swooping his son up to put him on his shoulders. "I'll even give you a ride to the bathroom. You brush your teeth, and after you've gone to sleep, Sue will drive us over to Leah's house."

"But I don't wanna—"

"Morning will be here before you know it if you go to sleep now," Sue assured him.

"Yeah, but—"

"No more buts," Jared reiterated, giving Tommy a bouncy ride to the doorway. "Say good night to everybody."

Pouting just a little, he did, and after saying good night to him in unison, Leah, Sue, and Jace exchanged amused glances.

"I bet he'll be awake with the chickens tomorrow," Leah commented. "I guess we just don't remember what it's like to be seven years old."

"Seven?" Jace wryly replied. "I hardly even remember what it's like to be thirty."

Leah poked him lightly in the ribs with her elbow while grinning at Sue. "He *is* getting old."

Nodding, Sue smiled back at her sister-in-law and brother. "Well, we're all going to be ancient before we know it—at least that's what Aunt Ellie tells me every time I see her or hear from her. She never fails to ask me when I'm going to stop wasting time and get married so I can start having babies. And I'm sure she's still after the two of you to start a family soon."

"Yes, and we just keep telling her we aren't in any rush," Jace answered, smiling indulgently, then glancing down at Leah. "I have to admit, though, I've been thinking more and more about a baby since Tommy's been here. He's a good kid."

"He has a terrific father," Sue said softly. "It can't be easy for Jared to have to raise him all alone."

Jace nodded. "That must be a job, all right. I admire him for doing it so well. You seem to be getting along with him, Sis. The two of you spend a lot of time together."

"He's a nice man. Intelligent, fun to be with."

92

Jace eyed her speculatively. "Sounds like Leah had a good idea when she decided to play matchmaker."

Sue just smiled mysteriously.

"Well, that was painless enough," Jared said as he reentered the study the following moment. "Tommy's all settled in his bed and—"

"Not quite," Sue corrected, pointing past him as his son appeared in the doorway in his blue pajamas.

As Jared turned around, Tommy smiled brightly. "I want a glass of water before I go to sleep, Daddy."

"All right, go get back in bed," his father patiently agreed. "I'll bring you some water."

Less than two minutes later Jared returned to the study once more, but he didn't have time to settle himself comfortably in the chair next to Sue's before Tommy appeared again, looking a little less sure of himself this time.

Jared tried not to laugh and succeeded. "Listen, young man, enough is enough."

"But Daddy, I forgot to leave milk and cookies for Santa Claus."

"But Santa's going to visit you at the other house," Sue interceded. "So you should leave him a snack there."

"She's right, sport," Jared readily agreed. "We have milk over there, and Leah will give us some cookies to take with us when we go over."

"But if I'm asleep then, you might forget."

"I won't forget." Jared shooed his son back out the door. "Now let's give this one more try." But when he returned to the den a few minutes later, he wryly announced, "Now he wants you to go tuck in him, Sue."

She laughed. "Determined not to go to sleep, isn't he? Any old excuse will do, even saying good night to me for the second time."

"That's part of it," Jared admitted, his darkening gaze holding hers. "But mostly he's found out how much he likes you and he can't really hide it anymore, even if he's not thrilled about us having a relationship."

"Ah well, you said he just has to get used to the idea," Sue murmured as Jace and Leah carried on their own private conversation while she walked to the door to stop in front of Jared. She smiled up at him. "At least he doesn't mind us being together. He just doesn't like to see us touch each other. We'll have to be patient, I guess."

"Yeah, take things slow and easy."

"Right," she agreed, then stepped past him. "I'll go tuck him in."

The bedroom door was open. The light left on in the bathroom across the hall cast a warm, comforting glow on Tommy's bed, and Sue could see he was waiting for her, half sitting up against his fluffed pillow. She persuaded him to lie all the way down and pulled the covers up to his chin, tucking them tight around him. "Night, Tommy."

"I'm not sleepy yet. Tell me a story."

"Oh no, I—"

"Just a little one. *Please?*"

"Okay, but it's going to be very short. Once there was a boy named Billy and he decided to stay up all night on Christmas so he could see Santa Claus when he came down the chimney. But do you know what happened?"

94

"Yes, Grandma told me this story. Santa doesn't come if you're awake."

"Well, Billy didn't believe that, but finally Billy couldn't stay awake any longer. Santa did come on his way back to the North Pole, but Billy was so tired and grumpy the next morning that he couldn't have any fun with his presents until after he'd had a long nap. He missed a lot of Christmas Day. You wouldn't want to do that, would you?"

Shaking his head, Tommy regarded her somberly. "Some boys at school say I'm a baby because I believe in Santa Claus. But I'm not a baby! He is real, isn't he?"

"In our hearts, he's very real. And you're not a baby," she answered reassuringly, tapping the end of his nose. "Now you've dawdled long enough. I want you to snuggle in. The sooner you go to sleep, the faster morning will come."

Tommy promptly squeezed his eyes shut.

Sue smiled down at him, then bent to kiss his cheek. When he made no move to resist her show of affection, she whispered, "Think you could kiss me back?"

Delighting her, he did so before wriggling down under the covers and bringing his worn security blanket closer to his face. With his fingers he found the corner he liked to stroke. He visibly relaxed, and within half a minute his slow, steady breathing told her he was fast asleep. She stood looking at him for a moment. No, he wasn't a baby. Perhaps he was somewhat immature for his age, but any child deserted by his mother could be.

Quietly she left him and went back to join Jared,

who was now alone in the den. She flashed him the victory sign. "He's out like a light."

"You're a miracle worker, unless you gave him a conk on the head."

"Nothing quite so drastic. I'm just a very persuasive woman."

"Mmm, I don't doubt that for a second."

"Meaning?"

"You know what I mean. Don't be coy."

"You be more specific."

"Later," he promised, smiling at their lighthearted banter. "First things first. I've asked Leah and Jace to keep their ears open in case Tommy wakes up while we're across the road playing Santa Claus. I think we'd better get the presents under the tree before taking him over there. Excited as he is, he'd probably hear us moving around downstairs and come to investigate. After we're finished, we'll come back to get him."

"You're a wise father."

"Of course," he said jokingly. "I'm pretty close to being a perfect fellow."

"And so humble," she retorted, grinning. "Where are Leah and Jace?"

"Leah's getting sugar cookies for Santa's snack, and Jace is putting the gifts I shipped down here into your car."

"Well, let's get going then," she suggested, leading the way to the kitchen.

While Jared put on his coat, she slipped into her jacket, then accepted the small bag of cookies Leah handed her. "I don't know how long it will take to get the presents under the tree, but I probably won't be back before you and Jace go to bed."

"Then we'll see you in the morning," Leah said quietly with a knowing smile. "I don't expect you to rush back over here when you can be with Jared over there."

"Hmmm, you *are* playing matchmaker, aren't you?"

"Yes."

"At least you're not trying to be sneaky about it," Sue said, then snapped her fingers. "Forgot something." She dashed to her room, took a gaily wrapped narrow package off the dresser, and slipped it into her jacket pocket as she hurried back to the kitchen, where she called good night to her brother, who had come back inside, gave Leah a wave, then rushed out to the car with Jared.

A few minutes later, in the house across the road, Jared got a blazing fire going in the fireplace while Sue poured a glass of milk in the kitchen, arranged cookies on a small plate, then carried both into the parlor.

Jared rose up from the hearth. "Oh, good, that's done. Tommy will be pleased to find the empty glass in the morning and the cookie crumbs on the plate."

Sue nodded as he walked over to cup her face in his hands.

She stretched up on tiptoe to kiss him lightly.

With a resigned sigh he put her away from him. "That had better wait, sweetheart. First things first. We have to get the gifts under the tree."

She nodded agreement, although the low tone of his deep voice had caused her pulse to accelerate.

Sue tried to slow its sudden rapid fluttering pace, but it was no easy accomplishment. Tonight he seemed more attractive than ever. In charcoal gray slacks and a black crew-neck sweater over a white shirt open at the collar, he looked casual and so at ease with himself, which merely accentuated his masculinity. Looking away from him, she sat down on the sofa, gesturing at the snack on the coffee table before her. "One of us is going to have to eat these cookies and drink the milk, you know."

"One of the sacred duties of playing Santa," Jared said, walking over to pick up one cookie, hand it to her, then take one for himself. "And since you volunteered to be my helper tonight, you have to do your part."

When both the glass and the plate were empty, Jared returned to the car for Tommy's presents. While he was gone, Sue took her gift for him out of her pocket and hid it among the packages already encircling the white-draped tree stand. Then she moved quickly back to the sofa when she heard him returning.

Laughing together, they began arranging Tommy's packages beneath the evergreen boughs. Thoroughly enjoying herself, Sue hummed "Jingle Bells" as she displayed the cowboy outfit Jared had bought in Fort Worth so that it would catch Tommy's eye first thing in the morning. While Jared set out a shining fleet of Matchbox construction vehicles, she wrapped a collector's case for Tommy's motor pool of miniature cars. And as he rearranged items to accommodate a mathematical computer game, he discovered the present she had hidden.

"What's this?"

"Oh, drat. You weren't supposed to find that until tomorrow morning. Just put it back where it was."

"No way. We've finished playing Santa Claus, and I think this is the best time for us to exchange gifts. Tomorrow everything's going to be very hectic."

"That's just an excuse. You can't wait; you're as bad as Tommy." She tried to snatch the narrow box away.

He held it behind his back.

They scuffled playfully for a minute or so until Sue was so helpless with laughter she couldn't fight him any longer. But she smiled indulgently at him. "Now I can see where your son got his personality. You're as excited about Christmas as he is, aren't you?"

"Almost," he admitted, his eyes warm as they gazed into hers. "Now are you going to let me open this?"

"If you insist."

"I do. And here's your present."

"Okay." Nodding, she accepted the square package he handed her. "But you open yours first, since it's your idea."

"Thank you," he said a few moments later, admiring the pen and pencil set.

"You're sure you like it? When I saw it in the store I thought it was perfect, but after I got it home I started wondering if you already have two or three sets just like it."

"I don't. In fact, I'm notorious for using pens with advertisements printed on them. This is a big step up. Thanks." Reaching out, he traced his fingertips over the back of her left hand, in which she held his gift for her. "It's your turn now. Open it."

She did, taking care with the gold foil paper and bright red bow. When she lifted the top of the square white box, she found a beautiful fur hat and stroked its sleek softness. "Oh, Jared, it's lovely."

"I know you probably won't need it often in Atlanta," he murmured, his gray eyes searching hers, "but I thought it might come in handy in New York if I can convince you to come up and see me a few times before winter's over. Think I might be able to?"

Sheer joy welled up in her. He really did want to see her again after the holidays ended. Realizing she had fallen in love with him had made Sue happy and fearful at the same time; she knew she didn't want their relationship to be a mere vacation fling for him. Jared's words were the assurance she needed.

Meeting his gaze directly, she nodded. "I'd love to see New York in the winter."

"And maybe you'd consider inviting me down to Georgia for a few weekends?"

"Consider yourself invited."

"I will," he whispered, wanting to take her in his arms and hold her close. He knew she'd deny it, but he thought she was beautiful and he admired her spirit.

Removing the hat from the square box she held, he lifted the tissue paper lining the bottom, picked up a smaller gift wrapped in silver foil, then handed it to her and watched as she opened it to find a fine-linked gold chain.

"Oh, Jared, I love it," she said, holding up the necklace. The multicolored lights of the Christmas tree danced on the polished links. Looking back up at

100

him, she shook her head. "It's beautiful, but you shouldn't have bought me two presents."

"Why not? I wanted to."

"But—"

"Hush," he softly commanded. "Put it on. No, better yet, let me."

He took the chain from her, and she lifted her hair off her neck as he leaned forward to fasten the clasp. His knuckles grazed her nape, creating warm tingles on her skin. He was close, very close, and she placed her hands on his shoulders and lightly touched her lips to his. "Thank you."

"Mmm, thank *you.*"

For an instant he seemed ready to take her in his arms, but he drew away instead. "I guess we'd better clean up this wrapping paper before we forget."

"Good idea. If Tommy saw it in the morning, he'd know we started the festivities without him and he wouldn't like that."

"You know my son very well."

"I know children," she corrected wryly. "And most of them want to be in the middle of anything that happens, especially something nice like opening gifts."

"Well, Tommy doesn't have to worry about being left out. Look at all the loot under that tree."

"How do you plan to get it all back to New York?"

Smiling wisely, Jared tapped a forefinger against his left temple. "I thought ahead and brought a nearly empty suitcase with me just to take his toys home in. I hope it will be big enough. This isn't all the stuff he'll be getting tomorrow. You'll give him the hat, and Leah and Jace bought him something."

101

"And some of the hands probably have presents for him too," Sue added. "They all love him. It's been a long time since there was a child on the ranch. They're going to miss him when you two leave."

"We'll be back. Tommy's already begging me to visit again next summer," Jared said as he bundled up the torn gift wrappings. After she gathered up a few tiny scraps he had missed, they stood together and went into the kitchen, where they discarded the evidence.

Jared nodded. "Okay, I think we're all ready for the big morning. How about a drink? I can offer you more than one choice tonight, since I borrowed a bottle of soda from Leah. What'll it be, Scotch and soda or water?"

"Soda, please but light on—"

"I know, light on the Scotch," he teased. "You always say that. I'm beginning to wonder if you're afraid I'm going to try to get you tipsy and have my way with you."

"Well, mah mama always told me to watch out for you Yankee men," Sue replied, exaggerating a Texas drawl. "Said ya'll are too fast, and sly as foxes."

"Did she really?" he asked, chuckling. "Isn't that a coincidence? My father always told me to watch out for 'little ole Texas gals,' because before you know what's hit you, one of them might have you roped and tied."

"I don't believe your father ever said any such thing."

"You're right, he didn't. But maybe he should have," was Jared's vague response before he playfully tweaked a strand of her hair, then went to the refrigerator to take out a tray of ice.

After they carried their drinks into the parlor and sat down together on the sofa, Jared switched off the lamp on the table beside him, leaving only the tree lights to illuminate the cozy room.

"Sorry I can't add more wood to the fire, but I had strict orders from Tommy not to," Jared told her. "He doesn't want to take any chances on Santa not being able to come down the chimney."

"I don't blame him. I'm sure we didn't take any chances when we were his age either."

A lengthy silence fell between them, but it was warm and comfortable. They spoke infrequently, and they both felt completely at ease, simply enjoying each other's company. It was enough for them to share the contentment of a quiet Christmas Eve.

The tree lights created an atmosphere that was almost hypnotizing, and Sue was unwilling to leave. But when she finished the last of her Scotch and soda and melted ice cubes clinked in her glass as she put it down, she remembered time was quickly passing.

"It's getting late," she murmured with a barely audible sigh. "I'd better go."

"Not yet," Jared murmured back, looking at his wristwatch. "It's a few minutes before twelve. Stay until midnight so we can see Christmas in together."

She inclined her head, more than glad to be with him as long as possible.

"Another drink?"

"No thanks, but go ahead if you'd like one."

"So polite," he whispered, reaching for her, gliding

his hands around her waist to draw her closer. "Come here, Susan."

She went without resistance, her heart performing crazy acrobatics as his inviting mouth hovered for an instant above her own.

Loving him, desiring him, Sue was intoxicated. Running her hands over the front of his black sweater, she curved them around the powerful column of his neck while her parting lips eagerly met the demanding pressure of his. A raw sensual excitement rushed over her when he cupped the taut sides of her breasts in his palms. In their mutual breathlessness, their tongues tangled together in an erotic encounter of pleasure that she knew deep inside was only a beginning.

CHAPTER SEVEN

"Sweet. You're so sweet," Jared whispered before kissing her again, then again. The tender force of his mouth gradually increased; their lips melded together, both of them giving and seeking as Sue lay down on the sofa cushions, pulling him down with her, her slender fingers running through his hair, arousing passion in him to a fever pitch. He moved above her, his left knee opening her legs a little as her skirt hiked up above her knees. When she trembled and ardently kissed him, his hands roamed down along her waist to the curves of her hips.

Her pulses pounding, Sue slipped her hands beneath his sweater and tugged his shirttail free from the waistband of his trousers, aching for the feel of his bare skin. Moving her fingers in lingering circles over the firm flesh of his back, she lightly explored his spine.

"Susan," he groaned, wanting her more than he'd wanted any woman. Her generously curved body

105

threatened to drive him wild with longing, and his hands around her waist pulled her upward against him. The soft yet resilient swell of her breasts yielded to his chest, and he could wait no longer to take off her white blouse.

"Oh, Jared," she gasped when he quickly pulled her silky camisole over her head and carelessly tossed it aside. Overwhelmed by emotion, she kissed him once more, her lips clinging to the sculpted shape of his as her heart hammered. The partial weight of his torso pressed her down into the sofa, and the male heat of him seemed to scorch her through her lacy bra.

"I have to see you, touch you all over," he declared huskily, his hands moving beneath her to unfasten the bra's back hooks. Slowly, making her wait, he pushed her straps off her shoulders and eased the undergarment off her, then tossed it aside too.

Feeling vulnerable in a most wonderful way, Sue caught her breath when she saw the unmistakable passion glinting in the depths of his gray eyes while his gaze drifted over her upper body to her face. Her eyes locked with his, and she trembled when he touched her breasts, his pleasantly rough fingertips caressing. He sought the peaks at last, teasing them with his thumbs, arousing them to swollen nubs. Her eyes fluttered shut as rapture washed over her. His thumbs still toying evocatively with her nipples, he cupped her breasts in his hands, squeezing gently, stroking, kindling an uncontrollable desire.

"Kiss me again," she whispered, her voice uneven as she allowed herself to drift deeper and deeper into the realm of sexual excitement.

His lips claimed hers, plundering their softness, devouring their sweetness as fiery pressure throbbed between his thighs when she sinuously moved one leg against him.

The indisputable evidence of his desire merely fanned the flames already burning in her. She loved him and was ready to give him that love. She took his sweater off, unbuttoned his shirt, then traced her hands over the muscular contours of his chest.

"Yes, oh *yes,*" she gasped when he released her mouth only to take the tip of one breast into his, tantalizing it with his tongue, exerting a tender pulling pressure that made her arch toward him eagerly. With his lips he played with one nipple, then its twin, again and again until piercing sensations were rioting through her.

He unbuttoned her waistband and started to lower her black wool skirt. She lifted her hips to make his task easier, feeling more alive than she ever had.

As he stroked her flat abdomen, his caresses burning through the fine fabric of her panties made her muscles flutter involuntarily. Aching for more kisses, never-ending kisses, she brushed her lips across his left cheek, finding his mouth.

Suddenly a shudder ran over him. He pulled back, cradling her face in his hands, his need smoldering like smoky gray coals in his eyes. "I need you," he said, his voice endearingly hoarse. "I'm sure you know that, but—I didn't come to Texas prepared for a romantic interlude. I want to make love with you, Susan, but I can't take the proper precautions."

A faint smile curved her lips as she gazed up at him. "It's okay. I'm on the pill."

Jared tensed. "Oh?"

"Not for the reason you're thinking," she said, lightly laughing as she shook her head. "It's just that I have a small problem and my doctor prescribed birth control pills to help it. It's okay."

"Is that your answer then?"

"What's the question?"

"You know what it is, you vixen. Will you come upstairs with me? Now?"

Powerless in the grip of the love she felt for him, she could only nod.

"Yes?"

"Yes," she said, winding her arms upward around his neck.

Sweeping her up in his arms, Jared carried her up the stairs, passing Tommy's empty room to enter his own, then pushed the door shut behind them with one foot. He carried her to his bed and laid her tenderly on the cover, then turned on the lamp on the nightstand. Warmth suffused her when his gaze wandered freely over her, taking in the rapid rise and fall of her breasts.

"Santa won't be using this chimney," he said softly. "Want me to start a fire?"

"No need. I'm very warm already."

"You're going to be even warmer," he promised. "So am I."

With his shirt unbuttoned and his sandy hair rumpled, he looked incredibly exciting. Anticipation stole over her as he removed his clothes, but when she visually explored his body, she felt a twinge of uncertainty that soon faded. Longing to be as close to him as possible, Sue reached out for him, wrapping her arms around his waist as he eased down beside her, his firm mouth seeking hers. She adored his touch and loved touching him. Enslaved by his lips, tempting him with her own, she ran her hands along his sides, then slipped them between their bodies to stroke his flat midriff, pleased by the responsive tensing of hard muscles beneath her fingertips.

"My sweet Susan," he whispered gruffly, his warm breath filling her mouth before he kissed her again. They were hungry for each other. Their lips met and parted time after time, merging in a succession of deepening kisses that weren't enough for either of them. As her fingers feathered his ears, he gently removed her panties, then stilled her hand as she started to switch off the lamp. "Leave it on, please? I want to see you, to look into your eyes when we—"

"Oh, Jared."

"You're shy?"

"Maybe a little," she confessed huskily, managing a tentative smile. "We really haven't known each other very long."

"Long enough, though. I feel close to you, like I've known you most of my life," he murmured, cradling her face in his hands, his expression tender. "And it seems like I've been waiting forever for this night, to be with you like this. I think you have too."

He was right, more so than he realized. And the affection and respect his tone conveyed erased all lingering doubts from her mind. Breathing deeply, she touched his beloved face, following the contours with a gentle caress.

He smiled. "Still feeling shy?"

"No. I . . ."

Satisfied, he silenced her with another kiss, catching the full curve of her lower lip between his teeth and coaxing her mouth open wider for the bold foray of his tongue. When the tip of her tongue scampered responsively along the edge of his, the marauding demand of his lips increased. Jared wondered if he'd ever be able to get enough of her. He doubted it.

"Susan." He groaned, his breath sweeping over her while he scattered wild kisses over her cheeks, her temples, her small strong chin. Tilting her head back on the pillow, he burrowed his face in her smooth ivory neck, inhaling the fresh fragrance of her light perfume, licking the racing pulsebeat he found.

Certain none of her initial shyness remained, he pulled back slightly and simply looked into her beautiful blue eyes for a long poignant moment, his gaze communicating passion tempered by all the tenderness he felt for her.

Lost in him, knowing the incredible power of love, she whispered his name when he trailed one lean finger over the natural arches of her eyebrows, creating currents of electricity with his light touch. A tremulous sigh of happiness parted her lips while a slow, disarming smile played over his. A wondrous understanding passed between them, equally shared, making them both realize they were meant to experience something rare and special together. No one in the world mattered except the two of them. No other place existed except this room.

Moving her hands over his broad chest, Sue detected the quickening, unsteady beat of his heart. "Kiss me some more," she breathed, her lips teasing his. His mouth covered hers with possessive force, tasting and relishing. He shuddered as her hands coursed down his back past his waist to cup his buttocks. With a low moan he leaned over her, rubbing his palms over her beautiful rosy-tipped breasts.

Parting her legs, he moved lower, scattering nibbling kisses across her abdomen, along her thighs, down her legs to her toes, which he nipped slowly, individually. Then his lips traveled back up again, grazing her soles, her ankles, the side swells of her calves before starting to torment her inner thighs.

She waited, waited for his intimate touch, and when he at last caressed her there, she felt she might faint with pleasure. She rubbed a silken leg slowly up and down his side, her heart filling with joy at the potent intensity of his response. Then he was poised above her, his gray eyes searching the depths of hers as he eased her knees wider as he lowered himself.

Feeling the pressure of him against her, she took a quick, hitching breath.

"Relax," he whispered, giving her a coaxing kiss. And with a tender thrust he entered her, capturing her first swift sigh in his mouth as she grasped the corded muscles of his shoulders. When her hands floated down his back, he moved slowly into her sheathing warmth, which blossomed open to receive him. Her dark blue eyes held his as he smiled softly. "Okay?"

"Wonderful."

"You feel so good, Susan," he said, his tone hushed. "So very good."

"You do too," she whispered.

With slow, rhythmic thrusting, he withdrew almost completely, then drove deep, again and again, never hurrying. He demanded much of her, expecting her to be a full participant in the loving, yet he was patient and gentle, making her love him all the more.

With his hands, his lips, his powerful body, he induced delight that heightened her need to give all of herself and to take from him. Time had no meaning. In a realm all their own, they moved in synchronization, soaring ever upward, seeking the heights. Her lips dallied with his; her tongue tantalized and aroused while the deep plunging flutters he created inside her came closer and closer, at last merging into a continuous, piercing tide. She gave a soft cry, borne up on a spire of physical bliss.

"Jared," she breathlessly sighed, tumbling over the edge into fulfillment more complete than any she had ever imagined. "Oh, yes."

"Susan," he groaned, moving faster, harder. He had wanted to continue loving her, to take her to the pinnacle of pleasure once again, but the delicious friction of her flesh against his was too compelling to resist any longer. Completion overtook him in a sweet, explosive rush.

Feeling his release, she held him closer, nuzzling her face in the hollow of his shoulder. His heart pounded as rapidly as hers; she could hear its strong thudding beat. As the tension in his long, lean body eased, she ran her nails lightly along his backbone.

A moment later they lay close together, sharing one pillow, their legs still entwined. While their breathing began to return to normal, Jared moved his hand over and around her torso, delighting in the silkiness of her skin.

Touching his face, Sue looked into his dark gray eyes. "Merry Christmas, Jared."

He chuckled. "I hope we've made it one you'll remember."

"I'm not likely to ever forget."

"Me either," he murmured, smoothing her tousled hair back from her cheeks. "In fact, you're making this the most memorable holiday I've had in years."

Pleased by his words, she smiled. Even now, with desire satisfied, she couldn't stop touching him. Tracing her fingers over his chest, she drew lazy circles on his damp skin until he lifted her hand to his mouth and pressed his lips against the center of her palm. In that instant her love for him knew no bounds.

Reaching down, Jared pulled up the top sheet to cover them. In the silent room they shared the warm glowing aftermath, exchanging kisses that were complete in themselves. After a while he heard the even tenor of her breathing and realized she was dozing off. Perilously close to falling asleep as well, he roused himself and raised up on one elbow. As he moved, Sue stirred against him.

"It's getting late," he murmured. "I'd better get back to the ranch and get Tommy."

She moaned sleepily. "Do you always toss women out of your bed in the middle of the night after you've had your way with them?"

"I don't take women to my bed. That's why Tommy can't understand my physical relationship with you," Jared snapped. "And his feelings have to

113

come first with me, so that's why I'm going to get him. Now."

Sue's eyes opened wide. Startled by his anger, she stared up at him. "I know we have to go back so you can get him," she said at last. "I'm not stupid. I'm sure Tommy expects to be alone with you in the morning when he gets up to see what's under the tree."

"Oh damn, I'm sorry I flew off the handle," he said softly. "I guess I'm just overprotective because Tommy's so vulnerable, so easily hurt."

"I know. I wouldn't ever do anything to hurt him if I could help it." Slipping out from under the covers, she got out of the bed and picked up her panties. "Most of my clothes are in the parlor. Do you have a robe I can wear downstairs?"

"I'll get them," he offered, swinging his feet onto the floor.

After he returned with her clothing, Sue quickly dressed while he did too. They said little to each other as they walked down the steps, through the kitchen, and out the side door to the car. Sue felt suddenly weary. The magic seemed to have gone out of the evening.

CHAPTER EIGHT

About nine-thirty on Christmas morning Tommy sauntered into the ranch house, wearing his new cowboy outfit and a proud grin. Smiling back, Leah, Jace, and Sue greeted him with admiring looks.

"Hey, those are fancy duds, Tommy. You look like a real cowpoke now," Sue told him. "Did santa bring you that?"

The boy shook his head. "It's my present from Daddy," he said as Jared stepped into the house. Tommy wrinkled his nose comically. "He forgot to get me a hat."

"You'll get one before we leave Texas," his father assured him. "I promised, didn't I?"

"Heavens, Jared, how could you forget the hat?" Leah joked. "That's the most important part of the outfit. I'm beginning to think you *are* a city slicker."

Laughing, Sue and Jared exchanged knowing glances.

With some urging Tommy told them everything

Santa Claus had brought him, but it was clear he was more interested in discovering exactly what was in the packages beneath Leah and Jace's tree. Everyone sat on the carpeted floor, chattering as they unwrapped gifts. Then Tommy silenced them all when he opened a box to find the hat Sue had bought him and gave a loud whoop he'd learned from the hands.

As he plopped the hat on his head, there were smiles all around. Watching his proud smile spread over his round face, Jared quietly suggested, "Don't you think you should thank Sue for that?"

Tommy did better, throwing his arms around Sue's neck and planting a damp kiss on her cheek. Hugging him back, she met Jared's eyes over the child's head as an intense happiness filled her soul. Not only did she love the man, she loved his son as well. And now it really did seem she was making progress with him, getting him to trust her.

Tommy even went so far as to give Leah a quick kiss when he opened the box containing the miniature farm she and Jace had given him. Complete with barn, tractor, animals, and a farm family, it thrilled him.

"It's not exactly a ranch," Jace said, chuckling as Tommy ran the tractor over the carpet, "but we thought it was close enough."

"It's great! Thanks."

Once all the gifts were open, Tommy had to see what everyone else had received. When Sue thanked him for the gloves she found under the tree from him and Jared, he spoke his mind as most young children are prone to do. "But you didn't give Daddy a present, Sue."

"Yes, she did," Jared said. "I opened it last night. It's a very nice pen and pencil set."

Tommy smiled, too excited to remember to protest being left out.

After a huge turkey dinner in the early afternoon, Jared was able to persuade Tommy to take an early nap. He went willingly down the hall, still strutting in his cowboy suit. Over coffee in the kitchen, Leah, Sue, and Jace relaxed. He thanked his sister for the movie cassette she had given him; Leah thanked her for the silk blouse.

"And thank you both for the beautiful gown and negligee. I love the ivory color," she responded, then took a deep breath to plunge right ahead. "I'm glad we're getting this chance to talk. I wanted to ask you guys if you'd mind keeping your ears open for Tommy after he goes to sleep here again tonight."

Jace nodded. "Sure we will. What plans have you and Jared made for the evening?"

"Oh, we're just going over to the house, and we'd like a little privacy."

A concerned frown creased Jace's forehead. "I see. Okay. I half expected this; Leah warned me it was probably coming," he said gruffly. "But I just want to ask you one thing: are you sure you know what you're doing?"

Sue answered honestly. "I love him."

"Does he love you?"

"He cares about me."

"That's not the same thing."

"Right now, it's enough."

"Are you sure?" Jace asked, his blue eyes dark with concern. "Damnit, Sue, I don't want you to get hurt.

117

Jared's a fine man. I like him, but if he causes you any pain—"

"Then I'll deal with it and survive," Sue softly interrupted, giving both him and Leah loving smiles. "I know you care about me and I'm glad you do, but I'm not a little girl anymore, Jace. I have to live my own life."

"I know," Jace muttered, then glanced at his wife. "I told you we shouldn't give her that nightgown; it's too damned sexy."

Leah patted his hand. "Sue's right. She's an adult. Lighten up, honey. You don't want to be an old poop."

Conversation ceased when Jared came back into the kitchen. For a long moment Jace simply glared at him; then Leah made some excuse to get her husband out of the room, leaving Sue and Jared alone.

"You told them," he guessed, sitting down at the table with her. He gave her a rueful smile. "Judging by the way Jace was looking at me, maybe I should be heading for the hills right now. Think he's gone to get his shotgun?"

Laughing, Sue shook her head. "He won't go that far. I'm glad I told him and Leah the truth. Sneaking around isn't my style."

"You are a very honest woman, which is one of the many things I like about you."

"Don't get the wrong idea now. I keep a few secrets," was her deliberate answer. "All women do. It's just that I want our relationship to be out in the open because I'm certainly not ashamed of it."

"It's good to know that," Jared murmured, then leaned forward to give her a lingering kiss.

After his nap Tommy played hard and made two visits to the bunkhouse to see the men. During dinner he couldn't stop yawning, and by eight o'clock he could barely keep his eyes open. When Jared carried him to bed, he didn't move except to hold his blanket closer.

Soon after Sue and Jared drove across the road. After hanging up their coats, he went into the parlor where she waited.

Sitting on the sofa, she handed him a glass. "Thought you might like a drink."

"Only if you're joining me."

"I have mine." She gestured toward her own glass on the end table. "But at the rate we're going, we're not going to finish the bottle before the holidays are over."

"Well, I still don't want to take it on the plane. Since you're driving back to Atlanta, why don't you take it home with you?" he suggested, laying a hand on her knee and smiling wickedly. "That way you can save it for the weekends I come see you. I wouldn't want you giving my expensive Scotch to another man."

"I'll try to remember that," she teased. "Of course, if someone devilishly handsome comes along . . ."

"Someone already has. Me."

"I might meet someone more handsome," she retorted, grinning as he gave the tip of her nose a tap with one finger.

They both sat back and relaxed, Jared stretching out his long legs. Sue had plugged in the tree lights and now, as she looked at them, she sighed rather wistfully. "Well, another Christmas is nearly over. And this one has been particularly nice, I think."

"I'd like to think I have something to do with your feeling that way."

"Maybe," she murmured, glancing at him and grinning again. "Tommy's made it a special time too. It's been great to have a child at the ranch for Christmas. Kids add a special magic to the day."

Taking a sip of his drink, Jared nodded in agreement. "Tommy was so full of excitement today, I think he could've made old Scrooge himself smile a little."

"I'm sure of it. He's such a sweetheart. Nobody can resist him."

"Except his own mother."

Regret darkened Sue's eyes. "I'm sorry, Jared. I didn't mean to—"

"I know you didn't," he said, laying one finger against her lips. "Maybe I'm a little too sensitive."

"You have every right to be. When Tommy hurts, you hurt, and his mother's rejection has caused him a lot of pain. But maybe he's beginning to realize all young women aren't like Paula. When he hugged me this morning, I felt like shouting for joy."

A tender smile touched Jared's lips. "I could tell how pleased you were."

"I felt like it was a real breakthrough."

"I think it was. He even kissed Leah, which is a big step in the right direction. Since he's starting to trust you, he feels like he doesn't have to be so suspicious of other women your age."

"I do think he's opening up to me more every day."

"Because you never push. You let him make all the first moves, and I'm grateful. But enough of that for now. I haven't had a chance to hug you all day, and dads need affection too," Jared said, setting his drink aside to curve his hands over her shoulders and pull her to him.

When her lips met his, her heart lurched wildly, and warmth washed over her when he ran his fingers through her hair, then enfolded her in his strong arms. She relaxed against him, pliant and happy as he turned her until she was half reclining across his muscled thighs. Hopelessly in love, she opened her mouth to the gentle, compelling pressure of his and shivered with delight as their tongues tangled.

Fiery-hot sensations surged through his bloodstream, gathering centrally with unrelenting pressure. He ached for her; his heart pounded and his senses roared. "Susan," he muttered hoarsely, tightening his embrace, holding her hard against him. "I need you so much."

When his questing fingers slipped beneath the hem of her sea-blue skirt and drifted upward between her thighs, she felt dizzy and stilled his hand with hers. "Whoa, wait a minute," she protested half-heartedly. "Remember the negligee Leah and Jace gave me this morning?"

"Sure . . . What about it?" he asked between deepening kisses.

Her breath caught. "Keep this up and I'll never have a chance to put it on. I sneaked it over here."

"It's very pretty, but why bother getting into it? I'll just have to take it right off."

"Sex fiend."

"Yes." He nibbled her neck. "With you, that's exactly what I am."

Minutes later he rose from the sofa and pulled her up with him. They walked up to his room together, and after shutting the door rushed back into each other's arms.

The next morning when Sue awoke, she lay gazing up at the ceiling of her old room for several minutes and wished she could have awakened beside Jared. It hadn't been easy for them to come back to the ranch to get Tommy last night; both of them would have preferred to spend the whole night together, but under the circumstances that had been impossible. They never would have been able to explain the situation to Tommy, and his feelings were too important to treat lightly.

Despite the frustration Sue felt amazingly content as she stretched and yawned in her bed, recalling the passionate hours they had shared. Her skin still tingled as if the imprint of his caresses were everlasting. For a long time she basked in the memory of kisses and words spoken in whispers. But, little by little, as she remembered, the need to see Jared right away intensified.

Humming, she lowered her feet to the cold floor, found her slippers, and slipped them on. After putting her robe on over the sexy nightgown Jared hadn't given her a chance to put on last night, she touched her toes a few times, then went into the bathroom.

Ten minutes later, after brushing her teeth and taking a quick shower, Sue dressed and combed her hair. When she entered the kitchen a moment later, she found Leah relaxing over a cup of coffee and announced, "I'm going to go over and surprise Jared and Tommy with a big breakfast."

"Ah-ha," her sister-in-law said. "You *are* serious about him, aren't you?"

"Very," Sue admitted, then grabbed her jacket on her way outside. Walking quickly across the road, she entered the house through the unlocked side door.

In the kitchen she sang an old love song and started water heating on a burner of the stove for the instant coffee Leah had provided. Opening the refrigerator, she found a quart of milk and nearly a dozen eggs her sister-in-law had also sent over in case Jared ever wanted a late-night snack or breakfast before he and Tommy walked over to the ranch. There was also a jar of homemade strawberry jam and two sticks of butter, and Sue found a loaf of whole wheat bread in the pantry.

While drinking her first cup of coffee, she got out a frying pan, turned another burner on low, and started melting thick slabs of butter, deciding she would go up and rouse Jared out of bed before she started scrambling the eggs. He could get Tommy up while she put several slices of bread in the toaster.

When Jared pushed open the kitchen door a minute or so later, Sue was at the stove, her back to him. Remembering how incredibly generous and ardent she had been last night, he smiled warmly to himself as his gaze traveled over her. Then, silently, he moved across the kitchen, stopped directly behind her, and reached around to put his hands over her eyes. "Guess who?"

123

She jumped a little, then relaxed, laughing softly. "Is it Santa Claus?"

"You got it," Jared said, turning her around to face him. "Just a lucky guess."

She looked up into his dark gray eyes.

Sliding one arm around her waist, he held her chin between his thumb and forefinger and kissed her.

She returned his kiss for several glorious moments until things seemed to be going rapidly out of control. Then she dragged her lips from his and wound her arms up around his neck, holding him close. He hugged her hard; she hugged him back, smiling happily as she opened her eyes and looked over his shoulder. It was then she saw Tommy standing in the doorway, his pajamas askew as he stared at them wide-eyed.

"Hi there, cowboy," she greeted him hopefully. "Ready for breakfast?"

"No! You stop that!" the boy cried. "Daddy! I told you not to do that!"

Jared's arms fell away from Sue. She stepped back from him, anguish flooding her face. He turned to look at his son.

"Just calm down and listen to me for—"

Tommy burst into tears, spun around, and ran back up the stairs. Exchanging a quick, worried glance, Sue and Jared went after him.

CHAPTER NINE

Jared went up the steps two at a time, Sue close on his heels. Tommy slammed his door shut in their faces, but they didn't let that stop them. Entering the child's room as he flung himself facedown across his unmade bed, they hurried to him, worried frowns creasing both their brows.

"What's the matter, Tommy?" Jared asked softly. "What are you crying about?"

With a muffled sob the little boy yanked the covers up over his head without answering the question.

Sue and Jared exchanged guilty looks as Tommy shot one hand out, groped around a little, then finally found his security blanket, which he dragged under the quilt with him.

Jared sat down on the edge of the bed and tried to ease the covers down, but when his son held on to them for dear life, he let go, shaking his head. "Okay, if you want to stay under there a few minutes, it's all right. But we'd still like to know what's wrong."

"If you don't tell us why you're upset, we can't do anything to help," Sue added, reaching down to place her hand on the child's back.

Flinching, he scuttled halfway across the mattress to get away from her.

She took a hasty step back and stared miserably at Jared. "Maybe I'd better leave," she quietly offered. "He might talk to you if I'm not here."

"Maybe that would be best."

Nodding, she left father and son alone together. Even after she left, Tommy didn't come out of his hiding place. His crying slowed to soft hiccuping sounds, and Jared gave him a few minutes to compose himself. "Come on out of there, sport," he said at last. "We don't keep secrets from each other, remember? So you know you can tell me exactly what's bothering you. Come on now."

Inch by inch the quilt moved down as Tommy turned over. Soon his fine pale gold hair appeared above the edge, then his forehead, and finally his entire face. His lower lip poked out in a pout, and as he rubbed his eyes with his fists, he sniffled.

"Hey, are you going to play peek-a-boo all day?" Jared teased, touching his son's small wrists, "or are you going to look at me?"

Tommy didn't smile as he dropped his hands, gripping his blanket tightly with one of them. "I don't want you to do that," he muttered, his watery eyes accusing. "I don't l-like it."

Jared eyed him speculatively. "Are you saying you don't like me to kiss Sue?"

"Yes," his son mumbled. "I don't want you to kiss her."

126

"Why not? I know you like Sue."

"Yes." Tommy took a swipe at his runny nose. "She's *my* friend. Can't be yours."

"Why not?"

" 'Cause."

" 'Cause why?"

"Just 'cause."

"That's not a real answer and you know it," Jared said patiently. "And I don't know why you're upset. Since you like Sue, don't you want me to like her too?"

"No," was the boy's immediate answer. "Don't you kiss her no more, Daddy."

Jared frowned. "But why don't you want me to like her, Tommy?"

"She's *my* friend," the boy repeated stubbornly. "I want her to like *me.*"

"She does, very much. But I don't understand why she can't like me, too, and I can't like her."

Shrugging, Tommy retreated into silence and stuck his thumb into his mouth, making Jared realize he was getting nowhere fast. He bent to give his son a kiss on the forehead. "Okay, we'll talk about this again later. Maybe after you've had breakfast you'll feel better. Right now I'm going to tell Sue why you were crying. I know she's worried about you."

Down in the kitchen Sue moved around restlessly, unable to sit as she racked her brain for some reason for Tommy's emotional outburst. Moving from the table to the counter and back again, she wondered why it upset him to find her in his father's arms. But she had no time to consider that mystery carefully because she soon heard Jared coming down the stairs.

When Jared walked in, she rushed over to him. "What's bothering him, Jared? Why is he reacting this way?"

Sighing, Jared touched her hair. "He wouldn't tell me exactly. But he seems to think you can't be my friend and his too."

"And what did you say to him?"

"That he should want us to like each other. He didn't buy that argument."

"Maybe he's just reaching that age when a boy begins to compete with his father for a woman's affection. I'm not saying he thinks of me as his mother, but I am the first young woman he's warmed up to since his mom left him, so maybe he feels like you're stealing me from him."

"Maybe that has something to do with his reaction," Jared conceded, thoughtfully rubbing his jaw. "But I have a feeling there's something he's not telling me, that there's more to it than that."

"Like what?"

"I wish to hell I knew."

Recognizing the painful confusion in his voice, Sue put her arms around him. "I'm sorry, Jared."

"Sorry for what? It's not your fault."

"I guess not, but I still feel guilty. Maybe I should go up and talk to him."

"I'm not sure right now's the best time," Jared murmured, distressed when he saw her face fall with disappointment. "Later today would be better, I think, after he's had a chance to calm down."

"You're right. I think it would be a good idea for

me just to go on over to the ranch now. You can turn the burner back on under the frying pan if you'd like eggs for breakfast. The butter's already melted."

When she started to walk away, he caught her by the hand to turn her back to face him, his gaze imprisoning hers as he softly said, "This doesn't change anything between us, Susan."

"Of course not. I know that," she replied, managing a smile when he tenderly kissed her lips. Yet as she buttoned her coat while walking back to the ranch, she wondered if she truly believed what he had said. Perhaps it was already changing, since they couldn't ignore his son's feelings. And at the mere thought of Tommy, tears sprang up in her eyes, blurring her vision. He was such an adorable, vulnerable boy, and he *had* been opening up to her. At that moment, though, she was afraid she might have lost all the ground she had previously gained with him.

Sue needn't have worried. For the next four days Tommy stuck to her like glue. Although she often tried to discuss her relationship with Jared, the child repeatedly ignored her and changed the subject as soon as he could. It was obvious he didn't want to talk about it, so she finally decided to let the matter ride. To her surprise, Tommy seemed to like her better than ever. He was more affectionate; his hugs came fairly frequently and he even kissed her three or four times. When he was alone with her, he seemed perfectly content. It was only when Jared joined them that he clammed up and began to pout, which became an effective way of keeping them apart. When he couldn't be with her, he stayed close to his father, as if he was keeping an eye one him and making sure he didn't get time to talk privately with Sue.

As much as Sue loved Tommy, she needed to be with Jared too. Alone. But there was no chance for that. At night when she drove them across the road to the other house, Tommy managed to stay awake and alert until she left to go back to the ranch. Tension mounted, and whenever her eyes met Jared's, she could tell he wanted to talk to her alone too. The days were passing too quickly; their vacations were ending. Soon he'd be flying back to New York and she'd be driving home to Atlanta. The distance between those two cities seemed to grow wider and wider.

Friday afternoon Jared found Sue alone in the den, reading. He stepped into the room and quickly closed the door behind him as she looked up from her book, surprised.

"Jared! How on earth did you get away from Tommy?"

"He wasn't able to take his nap with one eye open today. He's worn himself out staying up late to keep us apart," he explained, dropping down beside her on the sofa and raking his fingers through his hair. "I really didn't think he'd go on with this so long. I had hoped that after a couple of days we'd be able to ease him into accepting the fact that we want some time alone together, but it hasn't worked out that way."

Putting her book onto a nearby table, Sue sighed. "I just wish we knew why he feels the way he does about us. He loves you and he likes me, so why does he hate the idea of us liking each other? You said you thought it must be more than just his wanting us both all to himself. Have you figured out any other reason for the way he's acting?"

"Hell no, he shuts me out every time I try to talk to him about it. And I'm only a father—how the devil should I know what's going on in a seven-year-old's mind?"

"You can't blame yourself for that. All children can be secretive. Tommy's obviously trying to ignore the whole situation. He won't talk to me about it, either."

"He sure has turned himself into one tough little chaperon, hasn't he?" Jared asked rhetorically, shaking his head. He took her hand between both of his, playing idly with her fingers. "This is not at all what I had in mind for our last week together here."

She smiled faintly.

"But at least we're alone now," he murmured, lifting her hand to his mouth and pressing a kiss against her palm. "Maybe we should take full advantage of the fact and go riding."

His caress did wonderful things to her, and she really wanted to go for another ride with him in the quiet woods behind Leah's old house, but she shook her head at last. "I'd love to go, but I don't think we should leave. If Tommy woke up and found out we'd gone off together, he might get as upset as he did the other day. I don't want to risk that."

"Yeah. You're right," Jared reluctantly agreed, then drew her closer to him. "But since we are lucky enough to be alone, we might as well make the most of it."

"And what exactly do you have in mind, Mr. Ryder?"

131

"Um, a little of this." He kissed her, pulling her onto his lap. "And a little of that." He brushed one hand over her breasts. "And this . . ." His kiss deepened, his lips firm and warm and demanding.

Sue was happy to be close to him again. Tommy had kept them apart for four days that seemed more like four months, and now it was good to be held by him and to hold him once more. Relaxing against him, she kneaded the corded muscles in his shoulders.

Her softness, her sweet light fragrance, her ardent response nearly drove him mad. "God, I've missed you," he said with a groan, stroking her cheek. "I've missed everything we have together; I've missed having you in my bed."

"I've missed you too," she replied, kissing him again. He tasted of mint, and she gave all her love in an endless kiss that made both their hearts pound. Her breasts yielded to the firmness of his torso, but she ached to be even nearer.

Jared wrapped his arms tightly around her, stroking her back, exploring the delicate structure of her spine with wandering fingertips. Remembering what they had shared, he ached to spend long hours with her again, exploring all the pleasures. Recalling the soft light in her eyes when they had made love, he scattered urgent kisses along her slender neck to the hollow at the base of her throat. The fine-linked gold chain he had given her for Christmas held her warmth, and his lips traveled its circumference to her nape.

Trembling with delight, Sue unbuttoned his shirt, her fingers drifting inside over his hair-roughened chest while his hands moved up under her sweater, lingering on her bare midriff, then cupping her full, rounded breasts.

She gasped when he moved his thumbs in slow, erotic circles, his touch searing through the lace of her bra. A wild shiver of desire stampeded through her as his gentle yet possessive caresses aroused her, and she arched into him, encouraging him to continue.

As if he could stop. He couldn't. Holding her, touching her, kissing her meant everything to him, and he felt his self-control begin to collapse. Opening her mouth wider, he devoured the honey nectar within as his passion grew.

"Susan," he whispered roughly, tenderly catching her lower lip between his teeth.

She arched toward him again, her heart thundering and heat sweeping through her veins, weakening her arms and legs. When he unhooked the front closure of her bra and his hands explored her breasts, she felt dizzy for several seconds before she forced herself to halt the motion of his persuasive fingers.

"Whoa," she said with a sigh, dragging her mouth away from the enticing warmth of his. "We—we'd better stop this now before we forget where we are. Tommy might wake up and walk in here."

"He won't. He's fast asleep. Susan, I want you—*need* you."

His gruff tone was nearly her undoing. "I—want you too," she confessed. "But this isn't the right time or place. You know that."

"No, I don't."

"Yes, you do."

"Susan."

His lips claimed hers again, and she eagerly kissed him back for a brief instant before pulling away to shake her head. "Jared, not here. I can't. It's my brother's house. Leah and Tommy are here. I—I need more privacy."

His glinting gray eyes held hers. "We could go across the road."

She was tempted, but finally managed to say no. "What if Tommy was to wake up while we were there? We'd have another crisis to deal with."

"Why are you always right about everything, woman?" he asked, nuzzling his nose against her jaw. "I'm going to make all this up to you when I come to Atlanta."

She swallowed hard, suddenly swamped with nagging uncertainties about his feelings for her. When he raised his head to look at her, her gaze dropped to his open collar and the bronze skin over his collarbone. With one hand she gestured hesitantly. "Listen," she said, her voice low. "I know you said you'd come to see me in Atlanta but—but if you change your mind after you get back to New York, I want you to know that . . ."

Her words trailed off, and he scowled, his eyes growing cool. "Is that your way of telling me you don't want me to visit you?"

"No! Of course not. How could you think that?" she exclaimed, a troubled expression on her face. "It's just that I'm trying to give you a way out of all this—if you want it."

"Maybe you're the one who wants a way out," he suggested harshly, his lips thinning. "Maybe you're

134

the one with a change of heart and you've decided it's too much trouble to have a relationship with a man whose child creates complications."

"That's a nasty thing to say, especially when you know it isn't true," she retorted, angry color rising in her cheeks. "I've tried very hard to cope with Tommy's shenanigans."

"But you still get impatient with him?"

"Sometimes, yes. But so do you!"

"You're right, I do. I'm only human, but I'm more than willing to put up with any roadblocks he puts in my way. Maybe you're not."

"Oh Jared, I . . ." She stumbled over the words and couldn't generate the courage to express the true depth of her feelings. "I—care about you."

His hands around her waist loosened their tight grip. "I care about you too, Susan, very much. I just have to know if you want to see me again after we leave here."

"Th-that's up to you."

"And that's an evasive answer, damnit," he snapped, moving her off his lap with uncharacteristic force. He stood and glared down at her. "If you make up your mind before we both go home, just let me know."

A sob rose in Sue's throat as she watched him turn around and walk out of the den. The hot pressure of tears that needed to be shed gathered behind her eyes, but she refused to give in and let them flow. She had asked Jared for reassurances but he had given her none. Instead he had been hostile and had misinterpreted her every word. Or had he? Perhaps he had only pretended to, simply to make her feel the blame for their disintegrating relationship. Perhaps he had seen that as an easy way out and had taken it. The very idea caused a painful knot to gather in the center of her chest, and she flopped down on the sofa, burying her face in the pillow of her upraised arms.

Walking through the kitchen, Jared mumbled a curse under his breath. His jaw clenched, he shook his head. He had tried hard to make his marriage with Paula work, if only for Tommy's sake, but in the end she had proved how shallow she was by leaving him and deserting her only child without a backward glance. That experience hadn't increased his respect for women in general. But he had thought Susan was different. Now he wasn't sure. He only knew he wasn't about to chase after her; he'd had his fill of going out of his way to try to please any woman. If he meant anything at all to Susan, she was going to have to make the next move. It was that simple.

CHAPTER TEN

Sue couldn't stay at the ranch to celebrate New Year's Day. Since the holiday fell on Sunday and the Atlanta schools were scheduled to open on Monday, she had to start for home early Saturday morning. After getting her luggage into the trunk of her car, she went out to the bunkhouse to say good-bye to Buddy, Cookie, and the rest of the hands. When she came back outside, she discovered that Jared and Tommy had joined Leah and Jace to see her off. She smiled wistfully at all of them.

"Wish I could stay until tomorrow," she murmured, adjusting the scarf around her neck as the wind whipped her hair.

Hands stuffed in his jacket pockets, Jace looked up at the overcast sky. "Mean-looking clouds. Looks like we may be in for some snow or sleet," he said before focusing a stern gaze on her. "You don't have snow tires, so if you run into any bad weather, you stop right away and wait until the roads are cleared."

"I will. I promise."

"And don't try to drive all the way through, either. Stay at a motel tonight."

"Yes, Papa," she teased, putting her arms around him to give him a hug. Then she hugged Leah.

"Have a safe trip," her sister-in-law told her. "I put sandwiches and a tin of cookies in the car so you'll have something to munch along the way."

Smiling her thanks, Sue turned to Tommy and bent in front of him. "Okay, cowboy, let's have a great big bear hug so I'll feel warm all the way home."

Without hesitation the child complied, wrapping his arms so tightly around her neck she could scarcely breathe. When he released her several long moments later, she kissed his forehead. He kissed her cheek. Straightening, she finally faced Jared, wondering what he was thinking. His mysterious dark eyes gave nothing away. Since their encounter in the den, his son hadn't given them even a second alone together to try to make amends. Now, as Leah and Jace discreetly moved away, urging Tommy along with them, she felt the need to say something to keep their relationship from ending in such deadly silence. He simply looked at her as a wisp of hair blew across her mouth and she tucked it back behind her ear.

Her lips were dry. With the tip of her tongue she moistened them.

"Jared," she began softly, "I—"

"Wait, Sue, wait!" Tommy suddenly cried, diving between his father and her while interrupting her words. He managed to put more distance between them as he insisted on another hug and kiss.

"Can I come to Atlanta to see you?" he whispered in her ear after she lifted him off the ground. "Can I, Sue?"

"Sounds good to me," she whispered back. "But you'll have to get your dad to say yes."

"Sue says I can go to Atlanta to see her," the little boy blurted, wiggling out of her arms to tug his father's hand. "Can I go, Daddy?"

His gaze still on Sue's face, Jared shrugged noncommittally. "We'll have to wait and see about that, Tommy."

"Aww, she wants me to come. Can I, Daddy, can I? I'm big enough to go on an airplane by myself."

"You may not be old enough to do that yet," Sue interceded. "Maybe Jared could fly down with you."

"No." The child emphatically shook his head.

"We'll talk about this later," Jared decreed, silencing Tommy's attempted protest with a no-nonsense glance. Then he opened the car door for Susan and leaned down to look inside at her when she settled herself behind the steering wheel. His eyes held hers captive. "What were you starting to say?"

"Just that I—" she began once more, then heaved a barely audible sigh when Tommy poked his head under Jared's arm to grin at her. She lifted her hands in a resigned gesture. "This isn't the best time to finish it, Jared, as you can see. I'll write to you."

"Fine," was his toneless reply before he stepped back, taking Tommy with him, and closed the car door for her.

After buckling her seat belt, Sue turned the key in the ignition, waved to everybody, and started down the driveway, tears gathering in her eyes. As much as

139

she enjoyed her independent life in Atlanta, leaving the ranch always made her sad, especially after a fairly long visit. This time was worse. Not only was she leaving the old homestead, she was leaving Jared too. She loved him. And as she turned onto the road, she took one last look back, wondering if she'd ever see him again.

Nine days later Jared searched through folders in the metal file cabinet beside his desk. He cursed beneath his breath, and when his assistant, Rob, walked through the open doorway, he scowled at the younger man. "Where the hell's the Compton contract? Pete promised to sign it and send it to us right away. Where the devil is it?"

An easygoing fellow, Rob simply spread his hands out. "Hasn't arrived yet."

"Terrific." Jared frowned as he sat in his swivel chair. "You checked today's mail?"

"Just finished. The contract didn't come. But you know Pete."

"Damn right I do. He's never kept a promise in his life. Too busy chasing women. Get him on the phone, Rob. It's time I had another talk with him."

"Yes sir." Rob clicked his heels together and saluted, but grinned back over his shoulder as he started back out the door. "You know, Jared, you've been a pain to work with since you got back from your vacation, but no matter how bad you treat me, you're not going to get me to quit this job."

"Guess I'm stuck with you then," Jared responded, a wry smile moving his mouth despite the inner aggravation he felt that had nothing to do with his assistant.

After Rob walked out of sight, he hunkered down in his chair, thoughtfully rolling a pencil between his palms. Sue had said she would write, but he hadn't heard from her yet and he was beginning to think he never would. Several times he had decided just to forget her, but that feat was far from simple to accomplish, and not only because Tommy never let a day go by without mentioning her several times. He didn't need his son to remind him of her. During the day he thought about her too often; at night she was in his dreams. She was the kind of woman who made a lasting impression, and he wanted to hear from her, see her again, even though Tommy was determined to complicate their relationship. Together they could surely solve that problem, if she was willing to try. Unfortunately it was starting to look like she really didn't want to go to the trouble.

"Damn!" Jared said, slapping the flat of his hand so hard on his desktop that pencils and pens rattled in their holder. A minute later, when Rob put him through to Peter Compton, he barked at the man and made him swear he'd have the signed contracts in by the end of the week. After hanging up the phone, Jared shook his head. He had to get control of himself.

Pushing Susan out of his thoughts for the time being, Jared sat back and began to read the mail piled up on his desk. As his interest was being piqued by the premise of a new game program, his father appeared in the doorway.

141

"Too busy to talk?" Richard Ryder asked. "We can get together later if you are."

"No, come on in. Sit down. What's on your mind?"

"That's my question. What's on yours?" the older man retorted, taking the chair in front of the cluttered desk. The resemblance between his son and him was striking. He looked the way Jared probably would in thirty years—his sandy hair graying and thinner on top, but with the same intelligent gray eyes and sensitivity that gentled his features. Propping up his right ankle on his left knee, he smoothed his black sock while surveying Jared's face. "What's the problem? I hear you've terrorized most of the staff during the last week. And after your mother talked to you last night, she said you even snapped at her. What's the matter. Woman trouble?"

A semblance of a smile moved Jared's lips but never reached his eyes. "How'd you guess?"

"Anyone we know?"

"No. It's Leah's cousin, Sue. She was at the ranch while Tommy and I were there and, uh, we got involved."

"How involved?"

"Intimately involved."

"So what's the problem?"

"Tommy, for one thing. He likes Susan very much, but he doesn't want me to."

"Ah yes, she's the one he couldn't stop talking about this weekend," Richard murmured, nodding his head. "But since he likes her so much, why—"

"Hell, Dad, I wish I knew. He won't tell me. He just doesn't want us to have anything to do with each other."

142

"I'm sure you could change his mind with a little patience."

"Try telling Sue that."

Richard Ryder frowned. "Doesn't she like Tommy?"

"Sure. She loves him, but she's the one who suggested we not see each other again since our relationship upsets him," Jared said, his expression hardening. "And frankly, Dad, I'm in no mood to try to convince her otherwise. I had enough of trying to make things work out with Paula."

"Paula?" his father spat out, his mouth twisting derisively. "She's nothing like most women; not many mothers would leave behind a three-year-old child and never even try to see him again. I'm sure you learned your lesson with her, so I'm assuming Leah's cousin is nothing like the inimitable Paula."

"Nothing at all."

"Well then?"

"Well then, I guess I'll make the next move," Jared said, smiling. "I've been thinking about calling Susan for the past three days. Now I'm going to."

Nodding his approval, the elder Ryder rose to his feet and started out of the office.

"Dad," Jared called after him. "Thanks."

"For what?"

"For the nudge."

"You didn't need it," his father told him on his way out the door. "You'd already made up your mind to call her."

That was true. Jared knew it and smiled to himself while thumbing through the front pages of the phone book to find the area code for Atlanta. He reached for the receiver, then checked his watch and realized Sue wouldn't be home from school yet. Deciding to wait until the evening to call her from his apartment, he got back to work.

Less than an hour later Rob walked into Jared's office, clearing his throat as he approached the desk. "These are for you."

Jared looked up and shook his head as he stared at the vase of flowers Rob carried. "It must be a mistake. Nobody would send me those."

"No mistake, Jared. Somebody did."

"Who?"

"Well, I didn't read the card," Rob said, putting the vase down on the desk with a knowing grin. "Thought it was probably very personal."

Left alone again in his office, Jared looked at the small bouquet of red Shasta daisies, white carnations, and lush green ferns. A small envelope was attached to the plain white bow. He opened it. The message on the enclosed card was simple. It read: "If you're still interested . . ." then gave the Atlanta area code and a phone number.

Leaning back in his chair, Jared linked his hands under his head and smiled up at the ceiling.

When Sue's doorbell rang Friday evening, her heart seemed to do a full somersault. She smoothed the front of her forest green embroidered caftan as she went to the door. Smiling expectantly, she opened it and found Jared standing on the front porch. Beckoning him inside, she said softly, "You're right on time. No flight delays, huh?"

"I had a talk with the pilot. Told him I had a date at

144

seven-thirty and wanted to be punctual," he said, his gaze drifting slowly over her. Moving his left arm forward from behind his back, he gave her a single red silk rose. "I thought I'd be able to find real ones in the airport, but this was the best the gift shop could offer."

"Maybe this is better," she murmured, twirling the cloth-covered stem between her fingers. "It will last forever. Thanks, Jared."

"Thank you for the flowers you sent me. That bouquet was a very pleasant surprise."

"I'm glad. I guess some men would be embarrassed if they received flowers, but I didn't think you'd be."

"Not at all."

"I'm glad," she repeated, then realized they were still standing at the door and that she hadn't even told him to put his suitcase down. She was nervous; it seemed like such a long time since they'd seen each other, and when he had called Tuesday night to say he wanted to come down for the weekend, they had only talked for a few minutes. Now he was here, no more than two feet away, and it was a joy just to look at him. Composing herself, she took the leather-trimmed canvas bag from him and put it down on the floor. "Let's sit down," she suggested, leading the way across the living room to the sofa covered with beige linen with narrow pale blue stripes running through it.

"Nice room," Jared commented, looking around as they sat down side by side. "I like your house."

"Thanks. I do too. It's small—only four rooms—but it's big enough for me."

He nodded.

145

Then, as their eyes met again, they both burst out laughing at the same time. He reached for her and she went straight into his arms.

"Crazy," he said, his deep voice muffled in her thick hair. "We were acting like somebody set us up on a blind date and this is the first time we've ever seen each other. This is more like it."

"Mmm, much better."

"It just seems like it's been longer than two weeks since we were together."

"I know," she whispered, snuggling against him as he trailed warm kisses over her cheek toward the corner of her mouth. She turned her head slightly, her parted lips finding his. "Oh, Jared, I've missed you."

"Not as much as I've missed you."

"More."

"Impossible," he insisted, cupping her slender neck in his hands, the balls of his thumbs lifting her chin.

Loving him, she pressed closer as he kissed her and ran her fingers through his thick crisp hair while her tongue eagerly met the invasive push of his.

Awhile later he pulled back to say, "Now that we know where we stand, we can relax."

"Yes, so you might as well get comfortable," she murmured, loosening the knot of his burgundy tie. "Why don't you take that off? Your jacket too." After he quickly complied, she unfastened his collar button while he rolled up his sleeves. She smiled her approval. "Now you don't look like you're here for a business meeting."

He gave her a devilish look. "Business is the last thing on my mind, woman."

"Good." She tucked her legs up beside her on the cushion. "How's Tommy?"

"Fine. And before I forget, he was very excited about the letter he got from you Wednesday. It was nice of you to send it."

"I promised him I'd write," she answered as her expression sobered a little. "Does he know you're here with me?"

Jared shook his head, his own features tightening. "I had to lie to him about where I was going. I told him I had business in Washington."

"I had a feeling you were going to do something like that," she said. "I wish it didn't have to be this way. I feel like such a sneak, and I hate that."

Jared got halfway up. "Want me to leave?"

She pulled him back down. "Don't be silly. I'm glad you're here. I just wish you could have told him the truth."

"The time's not right yet."

"Will it ever be?"

"I think there's a good chance. It will take time, though, and a lot of patience." He caressed her cheek with the back of his hand. "His psychologist got him to talk about his objections to us having a relationship. Judging by a few of the things he said, she suspects he's afraid that if I'm involved with you, you might leave us both someday the way Paula did. Maybe he even blames me a little for her going away and never coming back to see him. And he doesn't want me to chase you off too."

"He actually told his psychologist that?"

147

"He hinted at it, and she read between the lines. Maybe it's an educated guess, but it makes sense."

"Then you were right," Sue mused. "You said it was more than him just wanting both of us all to himself, but I never imagined his feelings might be so complex."

"You're the first young woman he's let himself care about since Paula left. She was my wife, and when he saw me kissing you the way men kiss their wives, I guess he was afraid it would all lead to him being rejected again."

"Poor little fellow. We're going to have to convince him he has nothing to worry about."

"I can be reassuring, but *you're* going to have to convince him you deserve his trust more than Paula ever did," Jared corrected her softly, touching her hair. "Are you willing to try?"

"You know I am. I just don't know how to begin."

"Well, for starters, I thought you could fly up to New York next weekend and stay at our apartment," Jared suggested, cradling her jaw in one hand, his eyes holding hers prisoner as his tone lowered. "I believe you and I can have something very special together. I want the chance to find out."

Pure joy welled up in her heart as she nodded. "We've already made a great beginning."

"Now we have to include Tommy somehow, because if he's unhappy, I can't really be happy either."

"I know," she whispered, loving him all the more because his son's sense of well-being came first with him. This was the man she wanted to father her own children if she ever had any; no child could ask for more in a parent than Jared was able to give. As he

148

feathered a fingertip over her chin, she curved a hand around his wrist. "I'll call the airline first thing tomorrow and reserve a seat on the earliest flight to New York Friday evening."

He smiled at her. "I thought you'd say yes."

She made a face. "Pretty sure of yourself, aren't you?"

"More sure of you and your feelings for Tommy. And I'll pay your plane fare."

"No, you won't. You don't have to."

"Don't be so prudish," he teased, amusement lighting his eyes. "I wasn't making an illicit offer. If you're short of money . . ."

"I can handle it—this time anyway," she assured him. "But next time I may have to get a loan from you."

"I charge high interest."

"I'll still pay you back."

"Indeed you will, one way or another."

"Such innuendoes," she retorted, pretending to be shocked before she had to laugh. Reluctantly she put his hand away from her. "Some hostess I am. I haven't even offered you a drink. Would you like one?"

"Later."

"Something to eat then? I made shrimp salad this afternoon."

"They served a snack on the plane."

"Then you haven't had dinner. You must be hungry."

"Not for food. For you," he murmured roughly, his large hands running over the cotton sleeves of her caftan. "Do you have anything on under this, honey?"

"Yes," she breathed, her heart banging like a hammer in her chest. "Of course I do."

"Drat," he replied. "I was hoping you didn't."

"You think I'm easy or something?"

"Susan, you've never been easy," he assured her, moving his fingers across her shoulders to start on the single row of buttons along the front of the caftan. With some fumbling he managed to undo the first three, then whispered in her ear, "How many buttons does this thing have?"

"Lots. All the way down to the hem."

"Did you wear it tonight just to make me crazy?"

"Yes."

"Vixen." With one quick yank he tore the garment open. Buttons scattered everywhere, and he murmured his satisfaction. "I couldn't wait."

"You're going to have to sew all of them back on again."

"It'll be worth it."

Sue caught her breath as his fiery gaze wandered down from her face to the sheer pale green camisole she wore that didn't close completely in front and covered but didn't conceal the round outlines of her breasts. As he untied the three white ribbon closures, she skimmed her hands over his broad back, soaking up his vital heat through the fabric of his shirt. He pushed the caftan off her shoulders, she wiggled out of it, and he tossed it aside, then slowly opened the camisole.

"Lovely," he muttered, transfixed by the satiny texture of her skin. "You're so beautiful."

And beautiful was how she felt when he cupped her breasts, arousing her nipples to firm, erect tips.

Burning passion gathered deep within him, threatening to explode when she covered his hands with hers and pressed them harder, with tantalizing ardor, against her cushioned breasts. With gentle fingers he kneaded and explored even as he huskily asked, "Does this mean you're not going to send me to a hotel tonight?"

"How did you guess?" she breathed, reveling in his touch. Quickly, deftly, she unbuttoned his white shirt and took it off him to run her fingers over his chest, finding even more warmth for herself in the radiating essence of him.

With his eyes Jared caressed her. His fingers glided beneath the narrow straps of her camisole, and he rolled them down her arms to remove the garment completely. He touched her breasts again, hearing her catch her breath as his own accelerated.

"Jared," she said weakly when his strong arms tightened around her waist. He lowered her down on the sofa and bent over her, the compelling weight of his torso pressing her into the cushions. They kissed again and again while his searching hands explored her slender, shapely body and she explored him. His tongue flicked evocatively inside her mouth, and she ached for fulfillment.

"Let me look at you," he whispered gruffly, kneeling beside the sofa. She was beautiful. Her dreamy blue eyes, her dark hair brushing her bared shoulders, the half-shy, half-sensuous expression on her delicate features mesmerized him. Without touching her he continued to gaze down at her, and he saw faint color tinge her cheeks.

"You—you're making me feel so naked," she whispered.

"Not naked enough," he murmured, easing his fingers under the waistband of her pale green panties to pull them off. His passion soared as he surveyed her long elegant legs, slender waist, and full breasts. She was so maddeningly alluring. He could have taken her then and there but held back, wanting to go slowly, to make the night last and last. Finally he had to touch her again, and his fingers grazed lightly over her nipples before he turned aside to kiss her calves and the tops of her thighs, his lips lingering to nibble and nuzzle her firm flesh.

Wild and wonderful sensations spread all through her, and her hands urged him back up over her once more. She needed to caress him, too, to bask in his warmth, to explore the smooth plane of his back. With the heel of one hand she drew skittering circles around his navel, feeling the hard muscles of his abdomen contract and relax again and again until he groaned.

"Honey," he whispered, raising her arms above her head, holding both her wrists in one hand as his mouth sought the sweet firm undersides of her breasts, then ascended the swelling slopes to the ruched crests. His lips closed tenderly around one and then the other, his tongue flicking back and forth and around. He gently caught them between his teeth, tasting, toying, and making her gasp.

"Jared . . . you're driving me crazy."

"That's my plan," he declared, cupping one breast

in his free hand while his lips swept over every delicious inch of its resilient softness.

When he released her wrists, she put her arms around him, stroking his hair, his neck, his broad shoulders. As he continued the assault on her senses, she slid her fingers under his waistband to move them slowly around to the front of his trousers.

Again he groaned, his skin set ablaze everywhere she touched. When she unbuckled his belt, he muttered, "Now I'm the one going crazy."

"Good," she told him in a whisper, holding his face between her hands and slipping lower beneath him until their lips could meet once more. Her tongue lashed lovingly against his as she returned his plundering kisses. She felt so wondrously close to him, totally attuned to his feelings. What they shared was much more than mere physical pleasure. He was involved emotionally, as she was; the tender respect conveyed by his caresses seemed to tell her that, and she eagerly trusted her instincts. She loved him with all her heart and needed to believe he loved her in return—or was beginning to.

She linked her hands together across the small of his back, holding him even closer. "Take me now, Jared," she whispered in his ear.

"Oh God, I need to," he replied thickly. "But this couch leaves a lot to be desired. Where's your bedroom?"

When he rose to his feet, then swept her up in his arms, she moved one hand to the right. "At the end of the hall."

He carried her there, put her down near her bed, switched on the nightstand lamp, and tossed back the covers. Dropping onto the cool white sheet, he pulled her down above him, lifting her up just enough to kiss her neck, shoulders, and breasts. Her hands shaky, she finished undressing him.

He turned over and pulled her beneath him, his thighs pressing down to part hers. He remained poised above her, his arms extended as his hands rested near her shoulders. Her lovely blue eyes, open and honest and giving, met the smoldering coals deep in his. The coals ignited, flamed up in a fiery glint, and he could wait no longer.

"My Susan," he proclaimed, a small smile of triumph softening his carved lips as she arched up while he thrust in, entering her sleek warmth.

For several long moments neither of them moved. They simply clung to each other, content with that precious moment. His hard body filled the aching emptiness she had felt, and his affectionate gaze warmed her to the marrow of her bones.

The bliss he saw in her eyes evoked a tenderness in him he had never felt so strongly. Covering her lips with his, he began to stroke up and down slowly, and she moved easily with him. Whispering endearments, they loved languidly, enjoying each other to the fullest. With every passing moment their pleasure mounted, binding them closer spiritually as well as physically.

Together they were rising, rising in an uncontrollable whirlwind of ecstasy, and Sue felt incredibly alive and receptive to the deepening ripples of sensation Jared seemed to control completely. When he withdrew for a moment, it seemed to last an eternity, and she lightly swept her nails across his back.

"Jared," she implored, then sighed with renewed contentment as he united his body with hers again.

With a deep thrust he was suddenly still, but as her hips rose and fell rhythmically, he could control himself no longer. Her enclosing warmth became an irresistible friction that made his head swim.

"So giving, Susan," he groaned, stroking in and out once more. "You give so much."

And it pleased her to give and to take from him. She could feel his throbbing need for release and did everything to intensify it. They seemed to merge into a single soul, their hearts beating as one. His pleasure pleased her as much as hers pleased him. Fluttering sensations increased in frequency, coming faster and faster, darting through them.

"Yes!" she gasped, her heart pounding. "Don't stop."

"I won't. Can't," he mumbled, braced above her.

They soared together, ever upward until waves of delight pulsated through her, cresting again and again. Crying Jared's name, she felt his hot release inside her and held him tightly as he tensed, then trembled in her embrace.

Considerably later she stirred lazily in the circle of his arms and leaned back slightly to look up at him, smiling contentedly. "Are you hungry now?"

He nodded, smoothing her tangled hair. "As a matter of fact, I'm starved."

"Shrimp salad sound good? I bought a nice white wine to go with it."

"Sounds delicious," he said. "But maybe you'd better serve me here in bed, since you seduced me before I could unpack my suitcase and I don't have my robe."

"*I* seduced *you?*" she exclaimed, laughing and shaking her head. "Oh no, it was the other way around. And I'm not going to serve you dinner in bed. You'll just have to go get your robe."

He lifted one eyebrow. "Buck naked?"

"I'll close my eyes, I promise," Sue said, slipping off the edge of the bed to put on her blue velour robe. Glancing back over her left shoulder, she gave him a perky smile, then strolled out of the room.

Smiling to himself, Jared stretched contentedly before he, too, got out of the bed.

A short time later they sat in the tiny breakfast nook adjoining the kitchen, sharing the shrimp salad and sipping wine. Between bites they talked and laughed, and the meal lasted quite a while. After Jared refused a third refill of wine, Sue gathered their glasses and plates and carried them to the sink, but before she could finish running the hot water to wash them, he stepped up close behind her, his hands spanning her waist. He pushed her hair aside, uncovering the nape of her neck. When he lowered his head to trail kisses along her hairline, she pretended to be astounded and moved out of his reach.

Scarcely able to hold back a sensuous smile, she shook her head. "My goodness, I think you're insatiable."

"You're right," he replied as he moved toward her. "With you, that's exactly what I am."

Giggling, she spun on one heel and dashed out of the kitchen, only to be caught by him in the short hall between living room and bedrooms. His arms went around her, pulling her back against him. As she relaxed, he lifted her into his arms to take her back to her rumpled bed.

Laying her down with tender reverence, he lowered himself over her, his smoky eyes penetrating the glimmering blue depths of hers. He took a long, deep breath. "Susan," he said quietly, "I think I love you."

Her heart stopped, then started again in an uneven beat as she looked up at him. "You *think* you do?"

His lips caressed hers. "I'm almost sure I do."

"Jared," she whispered, unable to conceal the truth any longer, "I *know* I love you."

He kissed her again. "I hope so. But you're going to have to give me a little more time. Paula did a number on me, too, not just on Tommy. But if you can be patient with him, can you be patient with me for a while too?"

"Yes," she vowed as he turned onto his side and held her close to him. "How could I possibly say no? I do love you."

"My sweet Susan," he murmured, his arms tightening possessively around her.

CHAPTER ELEVEN

The terminal at La Guardia airport was busy Friday evening. Tommy held Jared's hand tightly as they threaded their way through the crowd. "Is she here yet, Daddy?" Tommy asked for the third time in less than two minutes. "Is she?"

Once again Jared checked the airline monitor suspended from the ceiling and saw that the estimated time of arrival of Sue's flight had been changed. "The plane's going to be a little late," he said, glancing at his wristwatch. "You're going to have to be patient about twenty more minutes. Think you can hold out that long, sport?"

Visibly disappointed, Tommy shrugged. "I wish she was here now."

"You wouldn't want her to jump out of the plane and try to fly here ahead of it, would you?" Jared teased, ruffling his son's hair. "She's not a bird; she can't fly."

"Supergirl does," Tommy answered, giggling. "Maybe Sue has some magic clothes and a cape too."

Jared grinned down at him. "I know you like her, but don't expect her to pick up any cars with one hand while she's here. Okay?"

"Okay," the boy agreed, giggling harder at the idea.

"Let's wait in here," Jared suggested, leading Tommy into a cafeteria. "Want something to drink? How about chocolate milk?"

"I like root beer."

The hopeful expression on Tommy's face was too cherubic to resist, and although Jared knew he was being conned, he agreed to the soda. After they went through the line and paid the cashier, they found a small unoccupied table. Sitting sideways, Tommy swung his legs up and down, eyeing his brand new blue and white sneakers as he worked busily at the straw in his ice-filled cup. Before his father could drink half his coffee, he was down to the last few drops of root beer. Sucking in his cheeks, he slurped noisily until Jared's disapproving frown put an end to his lapse of manners. With all the innocent aplomb only a child can employ, he announced, "I'm still thirsty."

"Then we'll find a water fountain in a minute," Jared replied, setting his coffee cup down on the table as his expression grew more serious. "I want to talk to you about Sue, Tommy. I know how excited you are that she's coming for the weekend, but I'm going to be very glad to see her, too, and I hope you've changed your mind about us liking each other."

"Let's buy her something." Ignoring Jared's words completely, Tommy wriggled off the edge of his chair and headed out of the cafeteria. "Over there's a store. I want a present for Sue. C'mon, Daddy."

Deciding not to press the issue, Jared followed and patiently accompanied his son up and down the aisles of the gift shop.

Ten minutes later Sue got off the plane and walked quickly along the glassed-in corridor toward the center of the terminal. Finally, beyond the arch of the metal detector, she saw Jared and Tommy waiting for her. Smiling at both of them, her heartbeat accelerating, she hurried through the security area and stooped with open arms as Tommy ran to greet her. A sudden shyness seemed to overcome him as he reached her. He shifted his eyes to one side for an instant until she took the initiative and gave him a big hug, then pulled back slightly. "What's this?" she asked jokingly. "Don't I get a kiss, cowboy? Or would you rather kiss your horse?"

The small boy's trilling laughter warmed her soul as he complied, pressing his soft lips against her cheek. "I don't have a horse, but I might get a pony this summer. Daddy said so."

"Hello, Jared," she said quietly, her eyes alight when he walked over to join them. Although it had only been five days since he'd left Atlanta, it seemed as if they had been separated much longer. Again, as always, simply seeing him was a pleasure. When he took both her hands in his and leaned forward to give her a light brief kiss, she longed to move closer to him.

She wasn't given a chance. Tommy quickly slipped

between them to offer her a small silver box adorned with a blue ribbon.

Opening it, Sue found a small crystal cat, the perfect facets that shaped it glimmering in the light. "Oh, how beautiful," she murmured, including both father and son in her glowing smile. "Thank you."

His gaze conveying a secret message, Jared nodded, then said softly, "Let's get your luggage."

They walked down the stairs to the baggage claim area, where Sue pointed out her small red leather suitcase as it moved past on the conveyor belt. After showing her claim check to an attendant, Jared carried the bag as they stepped out into the crisp night air. Tommy stayed close to her side as his father hailed a taxi, and when they got into the backseat, he sat between them.

"Ready for dinner?" Jared asked her as their driver steered the taxi down the thoroughfare leading away from the terminal. "I hope you're hungry."

"I'm hollow. They served dinner on the plane, but I passed it up since you promised to take me to a terrific restaurant."

On the way to Greenwich Village Tommy kept up a steady stream of chatter about Joey, his best friend at school, who had three gerbils and one turtle as pets. He'd named them all after G.I. Joe heroes, which made them even more impressive. Sue gained points by being able to discuss those heroes, knowledgeably, having learned about them from her students. Jared and Sue didn't have a chance to say more than a couple of words to each other throughout the entire ride, but after they entered the small, elegant restaurant later and he pulled out her chair

161

for her, he softly admonished, "You're not wearing the hat we gave you for Christmas. And I thought you liked it."

"I do. I have it with me," she informed him, smiling. "It'll keep me warm if we go for a long walk while I'm here."

"Tommy and I will show you the Village," he replied, sitting down as his son squirmed into a comfortable position in his own chair. "Right, sport?"

"I want Sue to go to Joey's house too," Tommy said. "She can see the gerbil I like the best—his name's Duke. She can even hold him."

Jared chuckled. "*If* she wants to. Some people don't like to touch anything that looks like a mouse."

"Oh, I don't mind," Sue assured the boy. "I think gerbils are cute."

"Then we'll try to drop by Joey's house for a few minutes if his mother doesn't mind," Jared promised while beckoning a waiter to the table. "Right now let's look at the menu and order dinner."

On Jared's recommendation, she chose the sole almandine, which turned out to be delicious. He had that also, and Tommy didn't let a few unmanageable noodles lessen his enjoyment of spaghetti and meatballs. Then he wolfed down a piece of cheesecake while Sue and Jared ended the meal with coffee. When he tried to hide a yawn behind his crumpled linen napkin, they exchanged glances and Jared asked for the check.

"We can walk to the apartment," he said as he got her suitcase from the coat check room and they left the restaurant. "It's only a few blocks."

Grinning, Sue replied, "You New Yorkers always

say that, but you forget to mention that every block is nine miles long. I've been here before and I know."

"We'll take a cab then."

"I'm just kidding," she murmured, touching his arm, her heart beating faster when he covered her hand with his. But then Tommy grabbed hold of her other hand and began pulling her along the sidewalk, giving her more details about Duke, the gerbil.

A frosty silver moon shone down on Gramercy Park, and the bare branches of the trees reached toward the sky. Enclosed by a dignified wrought-iron fence, the park lay silent in the night. Dry leaves rustled in a tumble on the deserted walkways, scattered by the chilly wind. A stately and peaceful place, it was an oasis of serenity in the boisterous city, and the golden glow of the lamplights illuminated empty benches and the glossy leaves of evergreen shrubs. Sue found the park charming, and when Jared opened the gate to one of the regal town houses that stood like sentinels around the square, she expressed her delight.

"You live here? Oh, this is really nice."

Shifting her suitcase from his right hand to his left, he opened the front door, bowed low from the waist, and asked Tommy to escort her in. They took an antique elevator, complete with intricately carved wainscotting, up to the third story, their ascent smooth and slow. Although many of the park houses had been converted to apartments, they had lost none of their former beauty and dignity, as she discovered when Jared ushered her into the living room of his apartment. Ornate moldings still adorned the high ceilings, and the walls were an oyster shell white, the perfect background for the paintings hung on them, which brightened the room with dashes of reds, greens, yellows, and blues. Two charcoal gray sofas faced each other, and with a pair of scarlet chairs, they formed a cozy nook. On a table topped with thick glass was a brass bowl filled with fresh fruit next to a rather untidy stack of magazines, one of them lying open, which added a homey touch. Around the colorful Persian rug, the hardwood floor gleamed in a rich buff, and Sue turned to Jared with a grin.

"I never imagined you were such a housekeeper," she said. "You must wax this floor at least twice a week."

"I can't take credit for that," he admitted with a quirk of his lips. "Edith comes in every day to clean and to be here when Tommy gets home from school. We couldn't get along without her."

"She makes good pies," Tommy added, leading Sue across the room to one of the sofas. As she sat down, he scurried over to an ebony cabinet, opened the double doors and pulled a box out before hurrying back. "Play a game with me, Sue."

"It's almost nine o'clock," Jared said, putting Sue's bag down. "Past your bedtime, Tommy."

His son scrunched up his face. "Aw, I'm not sleepy. One game, Daddy, please?"

"All right, but only one. I'll play too."

"No," Tommy quickly said, shaking his head while he opened the box. "You'll beat Sue. She doesn't know how to play. I'll show her."

Accepting his exclusion from the game with a shrug, Jared sat down to watch as Tommy told Sue the simple rules. On the board they moved two plastic cars along a winding road, both of them trying to reach the finish line first but occasionally having to detour on the way. Within fifteen minutes the race was over; with several lucky tosses of the dice Tommy easily won. But that wasn't enough. He wanted to play again.

"No," was Jared's firm answer. "I said you could play once and that's it. You have to go to bed. Now."

Stubbornly shaking his head, the boy started to set up the game again.

"We can play tomorrow," Sue diplomatically suggested as she scooped up the dice and dropped them back into the box. "It *is* time for you to go to sleep."

"Not tired."

Jared stood. "Let's go."

"No!"

"Yes. Now march down the hall, brush your teeth, and put on your pajamas. I'll tuck you in."

"You're mean, Daddy," Tommy wailed, clutching Sue's arm. "I don't like you!"

"You don't mean that," she murmured gently, patting his small hand. "I think you're just tired and that's making you act rude. Will you go to bed now if I tuck you in?"

"Will you tell me a story too?"

"A short one," she said, helping him off the sofa and glancing solemnly at Jared as Tommy led her out the door.

Less than ten minutes later she returned to the living room, where Jared sat waiting for her. He leaned forward on the sofa to pour two brandies and handed one to her as she sat down next to him.

"It looks like you've won him over completely. A few months ago I couldn't have imagined him wanting any young woman to put him to bed."

Sue's clear blue eyes met his. "Does that make you jealous?"

"Maybe a little," he confessed, a semblance of a smile on his mouth. Then he shook his head. "But not really. I'm glad he loves you and you love him."

"Yes, I do. And I love you too," she whispered, her pulses beginning to pound when he took the brandy glass from her and put it with his on the table in front of them. Then his arms went around her, and she put hers eagerly around him as their lips met. Mutual passion flared, wild and irresistible, but as their tongues tangled hungrily together, she suddenly tensed in his embrace. "What was that? Did you hear it?"

"I didn't hear anything," he muttered, forging a chain of kisses around her luscious neck. "It's just your imagination."

"But what if Tommy—"

"He was asleep when you left him, wasn't he?"

"Yes. But if he woke up and—"

"I'll go check on him," Jared said, releasing her with undisguised reluctance to leave. In less than a minute he was back, dropping down on the sofa to take her in his arms again. "He's fast asleep. Nothing to worry about."

Still, despite his reassurances, Sue couldn't quite relax. Jared's hands coursing over her, his tender caresses and arousing kisses made her ache to surrender to his lovemaking, yet somehow she couldn't.

166

Deep inside she knew she shouldn't; the time was wrong.

"Stop tempting me," she breathed, pulling away from him, meeting his smoldering gaze. "I think I'd better go to bed too. Alone."

"Susan."

"You asked me if I could be patient. Well, you have to be patient too," she told him, her voice uneven as she touched his face, then pulled her hands away. "We can't take a chance on Tommy finding us together. We said we'd give him time, and he's not ready for that yet."

"Damn, I know that," Jared said, his hands lingering on the soft swells of her breasts before he finally let her go, his eyes glinting with passion. "But I still need you."

"And I need you," she admitted while quickly rising to her feet. "But he's just a little boy, and right now we have to do what's best for him."

After picking up her suitcase, Jared escorted her down the hall to the second door on the right. He opened it, placed her bag on the floor inside the guest room, then left her on the threshold before he could change his mind about going in with her and taking her to bed with him. It wasn't easy to leave her.

The next morning Sue stretched lazily and started to get out of bed. As her toes touched the floor there was a knock on her door and Jared burst into the room, looking around as he raked his fingers through his hair.

"Has Tommy been in here?" he asked tersely, his jaw tight. "Have you seen him?"

"No, I just woke up," she answered, her eyes widening. "You mean you can't find him?"

"He's not in the apartment."

"Maybe he's visiting someone downstairs?"

"I doubt it, but I'd better check," Jared said on his way out. "Be right back."

While he was gone, she quickly brushed her teeth, combed her hair, and dressed. And when Jared finally returned alone, her face fell. "Oh, I hoped he was at one of your neighbors."

"No," Jared muttered, concern shadowing his features as he strode across the living room to the phone. "Maybe he's at Joey's. It's just around the corner—but he knows he's not supposed to go there by himself."

Nervously twisting her hands together, Sue watched and waited as Jared swiftly punched the numbers on the Touch-Tone dial.

"Hello, Lisa, it's Jared Ryder," he hastily announced. "Is Tommy there?"

"Why no," Joey's mother answered, her tone confused. "Should he be?"

Feeling as though a huge rock had lodged in the pit of his stomach, Jared gripped the receiver tightly. "No, he shouldn't be there, but I thought maybe he was. I can't find him."

"You mean he's missing?"

"He's not here."

"Oh, my God! Where could he be?"

"I'll find him," Jared declared, hearing the panic in Lisa's voice and trying to remain calm himself. "Will you keep an eye out for him and call me if he shows up?"

"Yes, of course, you know I will."

Nodding, forgetting even to say thanks, Jared hung up and turned toward Sue.

She hurried to him. "Maybe he went to the park. Can he go there by himself?"

"It's private. He'd have to have the key to get in." Opening an enamel box on the glass-top table, Jared shook his head. "The key's still here, so that's not where he went."

"Has he ever done this before?"

"For God's sake, no! He's only seven years old and he knows he's not supposed to leave this building without me or even to visit downstairs without permission."

"Then could he be hiding somewhere in the apartment? Children like to hide."

"Damnit, Susan, I've looked everywhere," he yelled. "He's not here."

Nodding, understanding how upset he was, she had to ask, "Don't you think we'd better call the police?"

His expression grim, Jared went back to the phone.

While he made the second call, Sue went to Tommy's bedroom without really knowing why. At the threshold she stood and looked in at the jumbled toys on the shelves lining one wall. A small pair of pajamas lay in a heap on the floor near the unmade bed. On impulse she went across the room to look in the closet, then spun around when she heard Jared coming.

169

"What did the police say?" she blurted the instant he walked through the door.

"The sergeant asked me if I knew how many people are reported missing every day in this city. But I started raising hell and reminded him of Tommy's age and that I know children can vanish in this country and never be heard from again."

"Oh, Jared, please don't think that way," Sue said hoarsely, taking his hands in hers. "Tommy hasn't vanished forever. We'll find him soon, I know we will. It would help, though, if the police would cooperate."

"The sergeant finally said he'd alert the patrol cars in this area to be on the lookout. He also asked me if it was possible that Tommy had run away, and I told him I couldn't think of any reason he'd do that."

Sue's face suddenly went pale as a horrifying thought struck home. "Oh no," she moaned, her eyes tortured as they met Jared's. "What if . . . Last night, when we were alone together in the living room and I thought I heard a noise, what if it *was* Tommy and he saw us kissing?"

"But I checked on him. He was asleep."

"He might have been playing possum. He could have run back to his room and gotten back in bed before you got there."

"He wouldn't run away without his blanket," said Jared, searching through the clothes, then slamming his fist on the bed. "It's not here."

"I noticed his cowboy suit is gone too. And the hat I gave him."

"I'm going out to look for him. You stay here and wait in case he decides to come back. And call Ser-

170

geant Wallinsky—the number's on the pad by the phone—tell him what Tommy's wearing. That'll help." On his way out the door Jared attempted a smile. "There can't be that many seven-year-old cowpokes roaming around the city. He should be easy for the police to find."

The following half-hour was the longest Sue had ever endured. After calling the sergeant, she paced back and forth through the apartment, a dread she couldn't control building in her. At last she wound up in the kitchen, where she made herself a cup of coffee. The silence surrounding her nearly drove her crazy; she wanted to hear Tommy giggling and Jared telling her everything was okay. But the silence continued. The phone didn't ring, and there was no knock on the door. Soon she couldn't get another tiny sip of coffee down. Feeling nauseous, she resumed her pacing again, talons of fear clawing deeper and deeper into the center of her chest. If something were to happen to Tommy . . . She shook her head, trying to banish such thoughts; they were too horrible to contemplate.

Unable to sit, she took a magazine off the coffee table in the living room and riffled through the pages, seeing only blurred pictures. Yet it was something to do with her hands, and at that moment she wished she smoked.

When the doorbell chimed a few minutes later she jumped, and her heart pounded as she ran over to throw the door open. A sob of relief escaped her lips when she saw a policeman with Tommy firmly in tow beside him. Dropping down on her knees, she pulled the boy into her arms, hugging him hard. "Tommy,

171

Tommy," she crooned throatily, "we've been so worried about you. Where have you been?"

He didn't answer her. The uniformed policeman did. "We spotted him walking about ten blocks from here, ma'am. Are you Mrs. Ryder?"

She shook her head. "No. I'm a friend. Jared, Tommy's father, is out looking for him right now, and he wanted me to stay here in case he came back." Standing and gripping Tommy's hand securely, she smiled tearfully at the officer. "Thank you so much for finding him. You just don't know—"

"Yes, I do," the policeman cut in, nodding. "My wife and I have two children. If one of them disappeared, we'd be climbing the walls too." He leaned down to look Tommy straight in the eye. "And you tell somebody where you're going next time, Roy Rogers."

After the officer left, Sue led Tommy to the sofa, where he plopped down close to the arm at the far end and refused to look at her. Heaving a sigh, she sat down on the edge of a cushion. "Tommy," she quietly began, "where were you going?"

He ducked his head.

She tried again. "You must have been going someplace. Where?"

Scrunching himself up in the corner of the sofa, he stuck his thumb in his mouth while his fingers stroked the favorite corner of his blanket.

She decided not to press him. Getting up, she went to the desk across the room, found a piece of paper, and wrote a brief note, which she left propped against the reading lamp. Then, after putting on her

172

coat, she took Tommy by the hand again and pulled him to his feet. "Come on, we're going to look for Jared. He's out there trying to find you and he's worried sick. If he gets back before we do, he'll see my note and know you're okay."

Still maintaining a sullen silence, Tommy dragged his feet as she led him across the room, but she was undaunted. Opening the door, she started out of the apartment, then stopped short when Jared stepped out of the elevator into the hall.

"Thank God!" he murmured, swooping his son up and carrying him back inside. For several minutes he simply held him while Sue stood close by. Then he eased Tommy's thumb out of his mouth and looked down at him. "Where were you going?"

"Grandma's."

"But Connecticut's a long way from here. You know that. Why were you going? Did you get back out of bed last night after Susan tucked you in?"

Sniffling and struggling hard, Tommy squirmed out of his father's arms and ran down the hall to his room. He slammed the door shut behind him.

Sue and Jared looked at each other. A muscle ticked rhythmically in his clenched jaw. "Well, there's our answer: he did see us last night. And, as much as I hate to say it, I think he's trying to manipulate us."

She looked down at the floor. "He's succeeding." Tears welled in her eyes. "Jared, I just can't stand to see him this upset. I think I'd better go back home today, as soon as I can get a flight."

"Go home? But you just got here last night."

"I know, but I think I should go now," she murmured, heading down the hall to the guest room, aware that he was following her. As she placed her suitcase on the chest at the foot of the bed and started repacking, he remained in the open doorway, watching.

"You're really leaving?" he finally asked, his tone brusque.

She nodded. "I think it's best. We can't go on this way. We're frustrated because we can't show affection for each other, and when we sneak around and do it and he sees us, he's miserable. Right now it's a no-win situation. Maybe later . . ."

"How much later?"

"As long as it takes, I guess."

"But right now you're cutting and running?"

"Well, I wouldn't call it that. I—"

"It sure seems easy for you women to run away when things get tough."

She spun to glare at him, her fists clenching at her sides. "Don't you dare try to compare me to Paula, Jared Ryder. She left you and Tommy and didn't give a damn who she hurt. *I'm* leaving because I don't want to cause anybody pain, especially your son."

"Okay, okay, I was out of line."

"Yes, you were. I just think you and Tommy should spend the rest of this weekend alone. Maybe you can reach some kind of understanding."

"But what if we can't?"

"Then—oh, hell, I don't know. We'll have to wait and see what happens, won't we?" Sue closed her

174

suitcase. "Would you call a taxi for me while I go in to say good-bye to Tommy?"

Jared allowed her to pass him in the doorway, his expression stony as he watched her walk to his son's door and knock.

CHAPTER TWELVE

Sprawled across his bed, Tommy lay staring at the ceiling. He didn't move a muscle when Sue sat down beside him.

"I'm sorry you thought you had to run away. That's never a good idea. You could've gotten hurt," she said softly. "And you scared your father and me very much. I hope you'll never do it again."

The boy shrugged.

"Well, I just came in to say good-bye. I've decided to go back home today instead of tomorrow."

" 'Cause I was bad?" Tommy spoke at last, his voice hushed. "Don't you like me?"

"Of course I do. I'm not leaving because I'm mad at you."

"But I was bad. That's why my mother went away."

"No, it isn't, Tommy. Who told you that?"

"N-nobody. I . . . ."

As Tommy sobbed, tears filled Sue's eyes, and she

pulled him onto her lap to cradle him against her. "That's not true, Tommy; I know it isn't. Your mother didn't leave because of you. It's just that sometimes mothers and fathers aren't happy together anymore, so they decide to live in different places. They don't do that because their children have been bad or they're mad at them. It's just something that happens because parents can't get along anymore. It's not your fault your mother left."

"R-really?"

Nodding, she added, "Just ask your daddy. Or your grandmother. They'll both tell you the same thing. It's the truth."

"If you're not mad at me, why are you going home?"

"Because I think you and Jared need to be by yourselves, maybe to talk about your feelings," she explained, stroking his fine hair. "I'm just leaving a day early, that's all."

" 'Cause you don't like me."

It was a statement, and she hastily reassured him. "Listen, I want you to know that when I love somebody, I always love that person. Nothing can make me stop, and I love you, Tommy. Nothing's ever going to change that. It's the way I am. I still write letters to friends I made in first grade, and I see them whenever I can. And we're friends, aren't we?"

"Yes."

"Then you'll never be able to get rid of me," she said, smiling down at him, taking a tissue from the dispenser on the nighttable so he could wipe his eyes and nose. "I'll write you letters, and we'll see each other."

"Promise?"

"Cross my heart," she vowed, doing just that.

Tommy's expression brightened considerably. "Will you come back next week?"

"No. It's your turn to visit me. Maybe next weekend or the one after that. We'll have lots of fun together."

"I hope Daddy will let me come by myself."

"So do I, because it's not easy for Jared and me to be together. And it won't be easy unless you change your mind about us," she said solemnly. "You see, your dad and I want to be friends, but you don't want us to be, so whenever we're together, we feel sad. It might be better if we just don't see each other. We don't want to make you unhappy. We both love you."

"Oh," was all Tommy said, but a thoughtful frown etched tiny lines in his forehead.

She gave him a kiss. "Well, I'd better go."

As she released him and stood, he tentatively touched her hand. "Can I really come to Atlanta?"

"I can't wait for you to," she declared, then snapped her fingers as an idea popped into her head. She walked over to his toy shelves. "Which one of these G.I. Joe men is your favorite?"

"Snake Eyes. I like his mask."

"I'm taking him home with me," she said, picking up the small plastic figure and grinning when Tommy gave her a startled look. She went back to him and removed the gold signet ring from her pinkie finger to place it in his chubby hand. "And I'm leaving this with you. Take good care of it. My father gave it to me a long time ago. If we trade things that mean a lot to us, we'll have to see each other again.

When you come to visit me, bring my ring and I'll give you back old Snakeskin here."

Tommy laughed. "Snake Eyes."

"Right," she said, bending to give him another kiss. "See you soon, cowboy."

He hugged her tight. "I love you."

"I'm glad," she murmured, her eyes misting again before he released her and she swiftly left.

In the living room Jared stood with his hands thrust into his trouser pockets. He had carried her suitcase from the guest room and placed it near the door. Sue glanced at it, then looked back at him, her heart aching. She didn't want to leave him, but there was no other choice. Until something changed.

"Well?" he asked gruffly, interrupting her thoughts. "Is he upset because you're leaving?"

"He was at first; then I explained that you two should be alone. I'm sure I finally convinced him I'll always love him, no matter what. I asked him to visit me in Atlanta, but I also told him you and I shouldn't see each other as long as he objects to us being together because that makes us unhappy."

Jared cocked one eyebrow. "How'd he react to that?"

"He seemed to think it over," she said, picking up her purse. "But Jared, he told me something disturbing. He believes his mother left because he was bad."

"Oh my God . . . But he's never said a word to me or his psychologist about feeling responsible for Paula deserting him."

"Some fears are too painful to talk about. He only admitted them to me because he was afraid I was leaving today because he'd been bad," said Sue, wincing when she heard the strident honking of a car horn on the street below. Her damp eyes met Jared's. "That must be my cab. I have to go."

"Susan," he whispered as she picked up her suitcase and hurried out the apartment door. He followed and saw her step into the elevator. Then she was gone, and he slammed one fist against the other palm as he stepped back into his apartment. But he closed the door quietly, having made a decision. It was time for him to have a heart-to-heart talk with his son. He called him out of his bedroom.

"Let's sit down. I want to talk to you," he announced, leading Tommy to the sofa. After they both were comfortably settled, he began. "There's a lot I have to say, Tommy. First, you were wrong to run away today. You could have gotten into big trouble."

Tommy ducked his head, but nodded. "I know. Sue told me."

"Do you promise never to run away again?"

"Yes."

"For running away today you need to be punished. No TV for a week."

"Aw, Daddy," the child started to protest, then sighed resignedly as if he realized that punishment was fair. "Okay."

"The second thing is even more important." Jared reached out to stroke Tommy's cheek. "Your mother did not leave us because you were bad. She left because she wanted another kind of life."

"I know. Sue told me," the little boy repeated, his wide eyes meeting his father's.

"And you believe her?"

"Yes."

"That means you trust her," Jared said softly. "And that's the other thing I want us to talk about. I know Sue told you she doesn't want me to come with you when you visit her because you don't want us to be together and that makes us feel bad. And I know you love Sue. But so do I and she loves me, which means we need to kiss and touch each other. That doesn't mean we don't love you too. You're growing up, Tommy. You still need your blanket to go to sleep and that's okay, but it's time for you to understand that you have to think about other people's feelings too. Only babies think about only their own feelings, and you're not a baby. I know that. So what do you say? Think you could share Susan with me, since I love her too and that would make me very happy?"

Comprehension dawned in Tommy's innocent eyes and he nodded. "Yes."

Jared hugged him. "You are a big boy," he praised him, warmed by the feel of his sturdy young body. "How would you like Sue to be your mother, young man?"

Tommy pulled back, surprise written on his small face. "Are you going to marry her, Daddy?"

"Do you want me to?"

"Yes," was the boy's immediate answer. "Marry Sue, Daddy. Marry Sue."

"I want to. But I haven't asked her yet. I just hope she'll say yes," Jared said as Tommy jumped excitedly in his arms. "I have a meeting Monday morning, but I can fly to Atlanta in the afternoon and see if she's willing to make us her family."

When Sue pulled into her driveway Monday evening and saw Jared sitting on her front steps, she wondered for a second if she were seeing a mirage. After blinking twice she realized he was really there, and she cut the engine, jumped out of her car, and rushed to him.

"Jared, why didn't you call and tell me you were coming?" she asked before he gave her a brief kiss. "Shouldn't you be working today?"

"I'm a vice-president; my father owns the company. Once in a while I take advantage of my position," he replied wryly. "Besides, Tommy wanted me to come."

"Tommy? But . . ."

Taking her keys from her hand, Jared unlocked her front door and entered her house behind her. When she turned to stare at him curiously, he reached for her.

"What's this all about?" she gasped as his lips slowly roamed over her neck. "Tommy really wanted you to come see me? What's going on? Tell me what's happened!"

"I had a man-to-man talk with my son, and he realizes now that he wants all of us to be happy. He's finally willing to share you with me. I can't promise he won't still be jealous once in a while, but we'll be able to handle that if you're willing to try."

"Oh Jared, you know I am! I just want us all to be happy together."

"Enough to take on a ready-made family?"

Sue's heart skipped with joy as she leaned back in his arms, her eyes searching the gray depths of his. "Are—is that a proposal?"

"Yes, that's exactly what it is," Jared murmured, taking a small jeweler's box from his jacket pocket. He opened it to reveal an oval diamond set in platinum and gold that sparkled brightly in the light. Then he dramatically dropped to one knee before her. "Marry me, Susan."

"Oh, get up, you crazy man," she lovingly commanded, urging him to his feet to wind her arms around him. "I love diamonds, so how can I possibly let this one out of my grasp? It's beautiful."

"You can't fool me, woman. It's not the diamond you want. It's me. You can't live without me. And I can't live without you," he admitted, lowering her left hand to slip the ring on her finger. "Now you've promised yourself to me. I know you want to finish out the school year here, so we'll get married this summer. That'll give Tommy more time to adjust completely to our relationship. And after we're married, you can get your teaching certificate in New York if you want to. Or you can change careers. You're a great storyteller. Maybe you should try to write children's books."

"You know, that's not a bad idea. I'll tell you a secret. Deep inside I've always had a desire to become an author."

"Then go for it."

"Maybe I will."

"Just think of the satisfaction you'd find. You could be a dream maker. But, then, you already are. You've made my dreams come true."

"Oh, I love you, Jared," she murmured, lost in his dark gaze. "I love you so very much."

"And I love you," he whispered back, his hands

spanning her waist. "I don't just *think* I do, I know it."

Happier than she ever had been, she smiled radiantly at him. "This calls for a celebration, and I still have the Scotch you gave me to bring home."

Jared shook his head. "No thanks."

"Brandy?"

"Later," he said gruffly, enfolding her in his warm embrace. "Right now all I want is a kiss."

She touched her lips to his, whispering, "I'm so happy."

"I love you, woman. It's going to be hard for me to wait until summer to marry you. Weekends aren't going to be nearly enough. I want you with me all the time."

She kissed his nose. "My sentiments exactly, Mr. Ryder."

"I hope you won't change your mind when I tell you that Paula called me last night," said Jared, his carved features tightening. "After all this time she's decided she wants to see Tommy again, which means she may complicate all our lives."

The news was both good and bad. "I'm not too surprised she asked to see him," Sue said. "Not many mothers can walk away from a child forever. You are going to let her visit him, aren't you?"

"I don't want to."

"I understand, but maybe it would be better for Tommy if he could see her once in a while. He's the one who's going to be hurt if he hates her for the rest of his life. He needs a relationship with her. She is his mother."

"You'd be a better one."

"And I'm going to try to be the best stepmother who ever lived. But nothing changes the fact that Paula gave birth to him, and I think we should encourage him to accept her as she is and love her as much as he can, for his own sake."

Sighing, Jared nodded. "You're right. But if she goes too far and tries to gain custody of him, she's going to have one hell of a fight on her hands. And I'll win."

"Did she mention wanting custody?"

"No, but Paula's always been full of surprises, most of them unpleasant."

"Well, if she ever does sue for custody, we'll fight her—*together*—and we'll win." Sue eyed him speculatively, "Hey, do you want to marry me just so you can tell a judge you've provided Tommy with a stepmother who loves him?"

"That's just one of the fringe benefits," Jared murmured, pulling her closer, his warm breath tickling her ear. And when she moved sensuously against him and her opening lips sought his, he tightened his arms around her.

Sweetly familiar passion engulfed both of them, and the need to come together and express their love physically grew irresistible. Sue strained closer to him, meeting the tender thrusts of his tongue with her own.

Her increasingly intimate caresses drove him over the brink of self-control. "Susan" he murmured, lifting her up to carry her to bed.

They undressed each other and made slow leisurely love, souls merging, senses spiraling, hearts thudding wildly in the joy of their union. At last free

185

to exchange words of love, knowing they were made for each other, they forged a wondrous bond of faith and trust and permanence more rewarding than either of them had ever imagined possible. When completion came in a sunburst of shared ecstasy, they clung together.

"Oh, I love you, Jared," she softly cried out, suspended on the pinnacle of fulfillment. Tears of pure bliss glistened in her eyes, and she held him fast against her.

A minute or so later they lay facing each other, warm contented gazes interlocked. She played her fingers over the fine hair on his chest, and he kissed away the droplets caught in her thick lashes.

He smiled tenderly at her. "I never knew how terrific it would be to fall in love. I'm lucky to have found you. So is Tommy."

Smiling back, she shook her head. "I'm the lucky one."

"That's true, too. My son and I are quite a catch for a spinster schoolmarm like you," he teased, laughing when she retaliated by poking her elbow against his ribs.

Unable to suppress a grin, Sue rolled over and reached for the phone on the nightstand.

"Who are you calling?"

"Leah and Jace, to tell them we're engaged."

"That can wait."

"But they'll be so pleased we're getting married."

"Not as pleased as I am," Jared whispered, brushing his hand up and down her arm until she turned back over to look at him, her blue eyes glowing. "Woman, you're the sexiest schoolmarm I've ever met, and I love you. You're mine now. Remember that. Except for Tommy, I didn't care at all when Paula left, but you're different. I'm never going to let you go."

"Don't even think about trying to get rid of me," she huskily warned, touching her lips to his. "Your father told you to watch out for us Texas gals and he was right. We know what we want—and I want you."

"Just what I needed to hear." Nuzzling her jaw, Jared pulled her closer. "Does this mean you're inviting me to spend the night with you?"

Laughing softly, she answered his question with a lingering kiss.

Rebels and outcasts, they fled halfway across the earth to settle the harsh Australian wastelands. Decades later—ennobled by love and strengthened by tragedy—they had transformed a wilderness into fertile land. And themselves into

The Australians

WILLIAM STUART LONG

THE EXILES, #1	12374-7-12	$3.95
THE SETTLERS, #2	17929-7-45	$3.95
THE TRAITORS, #3	18131-3-21	$3.95
THE EXPLORERS, #4	12391-7-29	$3.95
THE ADVENTURERS, #5	10330-4-40	$3.95
THE COLONISTS, #6	11342-3-21	$3.95